I0566308

A TIME TO DIE
THE CROCKETTS' WESTERN SAGA: 8

ROBERT VAUGHAN

WOLFPACK
PUBLISHING
— EST 2013 —

WOLFPACK
PUBLISHING
— EST 2013 —

Paperback Edition
Copyright © 2021 (As Revised) Robert Vaughan

All rights reserved. No part of this book may be reproduced by any means without the prior written consent of the publisher, other than brief quotes for reviews.

This book is a work of fiction. Any references to historical events, real people or real places are used fictitiously. Other names, characters, places and events are products of the author's imagination, and any resemblance to actual events, places or persons, living or dead, is entirely coincidental.

Published in the United States by Wolfpack Publishing, Las Vegas

Wolfpack Publishing
5130 S. Fort Apache Road, 215-380
Las Vegas, NV 89148

wolfpackpublishing.com

Paperback ISBN 978-1-64734-774-1
eBook ISBN 978-1-64734-773-4

A TIME TO DIE

Chapter One

Somewhere in the pre-dawn darkness a calf bawled anxiously and its mother answered. In the distance a coyote sent up its long, lonesome wail, while out in the pond, frogs thrummed their night song. The moon was a thin sliver of silver, but the night was alive with stars... from the very bright, shining lights all the way down to those stars that weren't visible as individual bodies at all, but whose glow added to the luminous powder that dusted the distant sky.

Around the milling shapes of shadows that made up the small herd rode three cowboys. One was much younger than the other two. Known as "nighthawks," their job was to keep watch over the herd during the night, then turn them over to the drovers in the morning for the short drive into the railhead at San Pedro.

The night had been long, and in order to stay awake

the three young men were engaged in conversation.

"What do you mean? Are you trying to tell me you've never even had a woman?" one of the older cowboys asked the youngest one.

The youngest cowboy, whose name was Archie, cleared his throat in embarrassment. "I'm only sixteen. I guess I ain't never give it that much thought."

"Why, boy, don't you know you can never be a man until you go upstairs at Big Sal's Place?"

"With Big Sal," the other added.

"With ... with Big Sal?" Archie asked in a plaintive voice that was decidedly void of any enthusiasm over the prospect.

"Hell yes, with Big Sal. Big Sal owns the place. That means ever'body who comes in there has to go with her first."

"Tell you what," the first cowboy said. "Why don't we ride into San Pedro first thing after we get off work? It'll be daytime, there won't hardly be nobody else there, an' we can have our pick."

"All except," the second cowboy insisted. "He has to go upstairs with Big Sal."

"Well, yeah, but then he can go upstairs with anyone he wants to."

"'Cept whoever me an' you has already took for our own selves."

The calf's call for his mother came again, this time with more insistence. The mother's answer had a degree of anxiousness to it.

"Sounds like one of 'em's wandered off," Archie said. "Maybe I'd better go find it."

"Hell, why bother? It'll find its own way back."

"I don't mind," Archie said, slapping his legs against the sides of his horse and riding off, disappearing in the darkness.

One of the cowboys laughed a low, knowing laugh. "If you ask me, Archie's just anxious to get away from us before we talk him into actually going upstairs with Big Sal."

"Who knows?" the other teased. "Maybe we can convince him she's just what he needs."

"I'd hate to see the fella that really needs her." Both cowboys laughed at their joke.

Suddenly, from the darkness came a loud, blood-curdling scream filled with such terror that both cowboys shivered all the way down to their boots.

"What the hell was that?"

They heard the sound of galloping hooves, then, from the darkness, Archie's horse, its nostrils flared wide and its eyes wild with terror, came running by them, its saddle empty.

"My God, where's Archie?"

"That was Archie that screamed!"

Though both were wearing guns, neither man was actually a gunman. Nevertheless, their friend was in trouble, and feeling the unfamiliar weight of pistols in their hand, they rode into the darkness, to his aid.

A moment later, gunshots erupted in the night, the muzzle-flashes lighting up the herd.

"Jesus! What's happening? Who is it? They're all around us!" one of the cowboys shouted in terror, firing his gun wildly in the dark.

The two young men tried to fight back but they were young, inexperienced, scared, and outnumbered. In less than a minute, both had been shot from their saddles and then the night grew still, save for the restless shuffle of the herd of cattle.

At some distance away from all this, a short but powerfully-built man sat on his horse with his hat pulled low over a bald head and browless eyes. Though he had put everything in motion, he had not personally taken part in the proceedings. Now one of the other men, with the smell of death still in his nostrils, rode up to him.

"That's it, Doran," the rider said. "We kilt all three of them cowboys and took a look all around the herd. There ain't no one else ridin' nighthawk."

"Good. Now take the cows," Doran ordered in a hoarse whisper.

Six weeks later, and forty miles south of San Pedro, Will and Gid Crockett stopped to give their horses a few minutes' rest. Gid took a long pull from his canteen, wiped the back of his hand across his mouth, recorked the canteen and hooked it over the pommel of his saddle.

"Say, Will, you remember how Mom used to fry pork chops, breaded in milk and biscuit crumbs? Then she'd serve 'em up with a side of turnip greens, swimming in bacon grease and doused with hot pepper sauce, and a mess of fried potatoes, with eggs scrambled in 'em. You remember that?"

Will chuckled. "Why, Gid, I'm hurt. The way you're talking makes me think you don't care much for what we've been eating lately."

"Eating?" Gid scoffed. "Are you calling what we've been doing eating? Far as I'm concerned, beans and jerky isn't eating."

"Then what is it?"

"It's just staying alive, that's all," Gid said. He climbed back onto his horse. "Staying alive," he repeated.

"You're just tired," Will suggested. "You'll feel better once we get into a town, sleep in a bed, and eat something that wasn't cooked over a trail fire."

"You got that right, Big Brother. I am tired, all right," Gid said.

Will and Gid had a right to be tired. They had been

on the trail for the better part of three weeks. It had been a long, hard ride, and both brothers were butt-sore and saddle-weary. But the tiredness went much deeper than mere trail weariness. It was a tiredness from which they would never get relief, for they were committed to a lifetime of living on the edge. Will and Gid Crockett belonged to that restless band of souls who were unable to pick up the peaceful lives they had known before the war.

They had ridden for the Missouri border ruffian, William C. Quantrill. Though Quantrill's irregulars were never fully accepted as an official part of the Confederate army, riding with his bunch had served Will and Gid well. That was because the Crockett brothers were motivated not so much by patriotism toward the Confederacy but by a blood-lust revenge against the Kansas Jayhawkers who had slaughtered their parents and burned their farm.

The boys got their revenge, but it had come at a high price. When the war was over the regular soldiers of blue and gray returned home. Not so the men who had ridden with Quantrill and Bloody Bill Anderson. They returned not as war heroes, but as wanted men.

Will and Gid Crockett got out of Missouri just ahead of a hangman's rope. They were now nomads, wandering through the West. They eyed every stranger suspiciously and entered each town with muscles tense, ready, if need be, for a lightning-fast draw and a deadly accurate shot.

Now, late in the afternoon of their twenty-first day on the trail, they approached the little town of Cochise Springs. It rose from the hot, sun-baked earth like a series of low lumps of clay and rock. Cochise Springs was a one-street town that had grown up at this location to take advantage of the only water in the area.

They surveyed the town as they rode in. Since the war there had been hundreds of towns like this, and there was almost an ethereal quality to them. Cochise Springs was like all the other towns, faced by houses of rip-sawed lumber, false-fronted businesses, and a few sod buildings.

It had rained earlier in the day, and the street was a quagmire. The mud, worked into the consistency of quicksand by horses' hooves, had mixed with the horse droppings to become one long, stinking, sucking pool of ooze. When the rain stopped, the sun, yellow and hot in its late afternoon transit, had begun the process of evaporation. The result was a foul miasma rising from the street.

The saloon wasn't hard to find. It was the biggest and grandest building in the entire town. Shadows gave the illusion of coolness inside the saloon, but it was only an illusion. The dozen and a half customers who were drinking had to keep their bandannas handy to wipe the sweat from their faces.

Anytime Will and Gid entered a strange saloon they

were on the alert, and this one was no different. As they surveyed the place, they did so with such calm that the average person would think it no more than a glance of idle curiosity. In reality, it was a very thorough appraisal of the room. They were checking out who was armed, what type of weapons they were carrying, and whether or not those who were armed were wearing their guns in such a way as to indicate that they knew how to use them.

They also checked to see if there was anyone they knew, or more specifically, if there was anyone who reacted as if they might know them. It was particularly important for them to pick out such people, for their reputations were such that there were many more people who knew them than they knew. And because their lives since the war had been as violent as during the war, there was nearly always someone gunning for them for one reason or another.

None of the drinkers seemed to pose a problem. From all they could tell, there were only cowboys and drifters here, and less than half of them were even wearing guns. A couple of the cowboys were wearing their guns low and kicked-out, gun-fighter style, but Will and Gid could tell at a glance that it was all for show. They were certain they had never used them for anything but target practice, and probably were not very successful at that.

The bartender stood at the end of the bar, wiping the used glasses with his stained apron, then setting them among the unused glasses. When he saw Will and Gid step up to the bar, he moved down toward them.

"What'll it be, gents?"

"Two beers," Will said. The bartender started to turn away.

"And I'll have the same," Gid added.

Smiling, the bartender nodded, then went to work filling the glasses from the barrel.

"I didn't see a hotel as I rode in," Will said.

"That's 'cause we ain't got one," the bartender answered. He cut his eyes upward. "Got some rooms upstairs though."

"How much?"

"Depends whether you want 'em for sleepin', or for sportin'."

"For sleeping."

"Three dollars."

"Three dollars?" Gid said. "That's a little high, isn't it? How much if we took them for sportin'?"

"Three dollars," the bartender replied.

"That's the same thing."

"Yep. Thing is, if you're sleepin' in 'em, they can't be used for sportin', and the girls will be losin' money."

"What do you say, Gid?" Will asked.

Gid sighed. "I don't plan to sleep on the ground tonight. I say we take it."

Chapter Two

Will finished his second beer.

"We'll have another," Gid said to the bartender.

"No, wait, not me," Will said.

Gid looked at him in surprise. "I never knew you to turn down a beer," he said.

"The beer will be here when I come back down," Will said. "In the meantime, I'm going to take a bath. I've got several days of trail stink on me."

"Yeah, I been meanin' to say something about that, Big Brother," Gid teased, making a face and waving his hand in front of his nose. "Why do you think I've been staying upwind from you?"

Will laughed. "You're one to talk. You could put a skunk to shame."

"That may be," Gid said, taking the fresh beer the bartender had put before him. "But I can live with my own smell. At least, 'till I have me a few more beers and get a little somethin' to eat."

Will laughed at his brother, then climbed the stairs to the room he had been told would be his for the night. From the red textured wallpaper and the pink flounced curtains, Will could see that this wasn't an ordinary room. There was also a wooden bathtub, and almost as soon as he had the door open, a hotel employee appeared with a bucket of hot water.

Ten minutes later little wisps of steam were rising from the tub as Will slipped down into it. Fifteen minutes later, with his skin red from the hot water and soapy scrub, he dried off and walked over to lay on the bed. Still naked from his bath, he crawled between the stiff, clean sheets. He was asleep in moments.

When he opened his eyes, much later, the room was dark. Something had awakened him, but as yet he didn't know what it was.

Then he heard a soft rattle of the doorknob. He was on his feet instantly, and like a stalking cat, moved to the side of the door. He cocked his pistol and held it at the ready. Still nude, he could feel an evening breeze pushing through the window, and the texture of the boards under feet. He was intensely alert, ready for anything.

Someone was breathing on the other side of the door. The hall lanterns were lit, and a sliver of light shot in under the door. From the saloon below, he could hear the nighttime revelry, a playing piano, and someone laughing.

Will waited.

The doorknob turned again and the door began to swing open, spilling an ever-widening wedge of light into the room.

Will watched the back of the door ease toward him.

A shadow filled the light, gliding in through the opening, backlit by the lantern on the wall in the hall beyond.

"What the hell?" Will whispered in surprise, letting his breath escape in a rush. The person trying to get into his room was a woman.

Will grabbed the woman's arm and pulled her inside. He closed the door quickly behind her, the motion pulling her against him. She let out a cry of alarm.

"Who are you?" Will asked, backing away from her.

"My name is Dora Walters," the woman replied in a frightened voice.

"What are you doing here, Dora?" Will asked. He lowered his pistol, but didn't put it away.

"I live here," Dora said. "This is my room."

Will stood quietly for a moment. He knew he had rented a sporting room, but he hadn't really considered the fact that he might be sharing it.

"Oh," Will said, sheepishly.

"I'm sorry if I startled you," Dora said. She smiled. "But

I really didn't expect to find you like this." She looked pointedly at Will's nudity.

Will shrugged, then backed into the shadows and wrapped himself in a bed sheet.

"You're lucky I'm not the kind that shoots first," Will said. "You could've gotten yourself killed, real easy. Did you know that?"

Dora shook her head. "I'm sorry," she said. "I guess I just didn't think. I wanted to see you...." she paused in mid-sentence, then laughed, a small, throaty laugh. "I just didn't plan to see so much of you," she added.

Will chuckled. "I guess you did see more than you bargained for," he said. "Why did you want to see me?"

"Downstairs they are saying that you and the other one, the big man who came with you, are supposed to be very good with guns. Is that true?"

Will nodded. "We have some experience with them."

"I would like to hire you. Both of you."

"Hire us? Hire us for what?"

"To find the man who killed my brother," Dora said.

"Do you have any idea who did it?"

Dora shook her head. "Cattle rustlers, but I don't know who they were. All I know is that Archie, and the two cowboys with him, were murdered, and the cows they were watching were stolen."

"I wish I could help you, Dora. But what you need is a

lawman, and I'm not in the lawman business."

Dora sighed. "I was sort of hoping that since you and Mr. Chamberlain knew each other during the war, you might be willing to help him, if not me."

"Chamberlain? Noah Chamberlain?"

Dora nodded her head.

"What does he have to do with it?"

"He owns the ranch where my brother and the other two cowboys worked," Dora said. "When I went to the funeral, I asked Mr. Chamberlain if he had any idea who killed Archie. He said he knew who it was. He said everyone knew who it was. It was an outlaw named Rollo Doran. Doran has been harassing all the ranchers in the valley."

"If they know who it is, why doesn't the law arrest him?"

"I asked Mr. Chamberlain that. He said it was more than the marshal could handle. He said it would take someone like you and your brother."

"I don't know why he would say that," Will said. "We aren't lawmen, and we certainly aren't vigilantes."

"He didn't say you were. It was my idea to try and hire you. Especially after all the things he said about you."

"What did he say about my brother and me?"

"He said that he had met you during the war, and he considered you to be honorable men. I was hoping that maybe, because you were friends, you would..."

"We were not friends," Will said, interrupting her.

Dora looked confused. "You mean you didn't know him?"

"We knew him, all right. We just weren't friends."

"I don't understand."

"Easy enough to understand," Will said. "Noah Chamberlain fought for the North, my brother and I fought for the South. We were enemies."

"Enemies? And yet, he thinks so highly of you," Dora said. "How odd."

"It isn't all that odd if you understand war," Will said. He paused for a moment. "My brother and I were planning to go through San Pedro anyway. Maybe we'll stop by and visit Chamberlain."

"Oh, thank you!" Dora said.

Will shook his head and held up his hand. "I'm not agreeing to anything," he said. "I just said I'll stop by and have a visit with Chamberlain."

"That's enough for me," Dora said. "If you are honorable men, as Mr. Chamberlain says, then I know you will do the right thing." She stood there for a long moment, looking at Will. Then she laughed.

"What is it?"

"Wrapped up in that bed sheet the way you are, you look like one of those Roman senators."

Will looked down at himself. "Yeah, I guess I do at that," he said, chuckling.

"Well, I can't stay here," she said. "I've got work to do."

"What the hell? You won't be bringing anyone in here?" Will asked.

Dora laughed at the idea. "Now, that would make a pretty picture, wouldn't it? Me and a gentleman in bed and you sitting over on the chair waiting until we were finished." She laughed again.

"I don't think it's a damn bit funny," Will said.

Dora smiled at him. "Don't worry," she said. "We have rooms at the far end of the hall for the short dates. This room is only for over-nighters ... which actually you are." She leaned over and kissed him on the forehead. "I'll see you at eleven."

"You're coming back?"

"Yes, of course. I sleep here, remember? That is, if you let me sleep," she added in a husky voice.

"You can sleep in the daytime," Will said.

Dora paused in the door and looked back. "I suppose I could at that," she said.

Downstairs, Gid, fed and with his thirst satisfied, had forgotten all about bed. He was playing poker, and it was one of those nights when everything was going right. He could almost will the cards he needed into his hand.

Holding a pair of jacks, he had just called for three more cards. When he picked up two more jacks, it was all he could do to keep the smile off his face. It was his bet.

"Five dollars," he said.

"Mister, I think you're bluffing," one of the other players said with an expression of confidence on his face. "I'm going to raise that to twenty-five dollars."

Now, Gid made no attempt whatever to keep the smile off his face.

"Let's bump it up to a hundred," he said, sliding the money to the center of the table.

The player who had called his bluff knew he had stepped into it, and the expression of confidence was replaced by one of chagrin. He started to call Gid, but thought better of it.

"It's your pot," he said.

Chapter Three

San Pedro was a good forty miles west, and though the boys could have ridden their horses, Gid's poker winnings enabled them to take the train. They arranged to have their horses shipped in the stock car, while they took a seat in the day coach. It was an easy way to travel and they sat looking out the window of the train as the terrain rolled by.

True to her promise, Dora had returned at eleven the night before. But finding Will asleep, and being tired herself, she had merely slipped into bed beside him. When Will woke up that morning, he'd left without waking her.

He did think about what she had told him though. It had been interesting to learn about what had happened to Lieutenant Noah Chamberlain since the war's end. Will leaned back in his seat, propped his knees up on the seat-back before him, tipped his hat down over his eyes, and drifted off to another time, remembering a battle that was fought long ago, and far away.

Because of the ebb and flow of the battle, the dead and wounded were scattered over a wide area. The fighting had left many casualties on both sides, and during the night their moans and cries could be heard even above the thunderous drumming of the rain and the incessant boom of artillery. The sound was heart-rending, even to the most hardened ears.

Most of the wounded were calling for water, so Will and Gid collected half a dozen canteens and started out onto the battlefield. Fortunately, the rain stopped shortly after they went out, but the night was still dark and overcast, without moon or stars to light the way.

Will and Gid weren't the only ones who went out, and because the night was so dark, many of the men who prowled the battleground were carrying lanterns to help them distinguish the wounded from the dead. As a result, the battlefield looked like a great meadow filled with giant fireflies, with the lanterns bobbing about from point to point.

A breeze came up, carrying on its breath a damp chill. Will pulled his coat about him and continued on his mission of mercy, picking his way across roads and fields, now littered with the residue of battle: weapons, equipment, and among the discards, the dead and dying.

"Water," a weak voice called, and Will halted. "I beg of you, sir, be you Union or Reb, if you are a God-fearing man, you'll give me water."

"Yes," Will said. "I have water." Moving quickly to the soldier, he saw that it was a Yankee officer, an infantry lieutenant. He uncorked the canteen and knelt down by the officer, then lifted his head.

"Here you go, Yank," he said.

"Bless you," the wounded soldier replied.

Will heard the metallic click of a pistol being cocked.

"Don't go wasting water on that Yank. I'm about to kill him," a cold voice said.

Will looked toward the man who had spoken and saw a Confederate officer. The officer was quite small for a full-grown man. He was just over five-feet-two inches tall, and couldn't have weighed more than 125 pounds. He had blotchy red skin, watery blue eyes, and a large, beak-like nose. Will didn't recognize him, but that was understandable, as there had been thousands of men from both sides committed to this fight. There was no way Will could know everyone.

"I'm not going to deny this man a drink of water just because he's wearing a blue uniform," Will said.

"Don't think that because you're wearing gray I

won't shoot you," the Confederate officer replied. "As far as I'm concerned, he and all the rest of the Yankee trash out here can die of thirst, and I'll shoot anyone who tries to help them."

"If you are going to shoot, go ahead and shoot," Will said resolutely. "But this man's going to have water on his lips when we die." Once again, he turned the canteen up to the Yankee officer's lips, and the wounded man began drinking thirstily.

"You son of a bitch! I warned you!" the Confederate officer shouted. That was as far as he got. An instant before he could pull the trigger, there was a rather solid-sounding thump as Gid, who had come up behind him, hit him over the head.

"Did you kill him?" Will asked. There was nonchalance to his voice that belied the situation.

"No," Gid said, kneeling down beside the man he had just hit. "He's still alive, but he's going to have one hell of a headache when he wakes up."

"Thank you," the wounded Yankee said, as he took his fill of water. "You are a true gentleman." Seeing Gid come over to join them, the young officer added. "Both of you."

"Where are you hit?" Will asked.

"In the leg."

Will held the lantern down toward the wound as he and Gid examined it. "What do you think, Gid?"

"The bleeding has pretty much stopped. I think if he can get back to his surgeon and have the bullet taken out before it festers, he'll be all right," Gid said.

"You think you can walk?" Will asked.

"I don't know. I'll try."

"We'll help."

With Will on one side and Gid on the other, they got the young officer on his feet, then began walking him toward the Union lines.

"My name is Chamberlain," the young officer said. "Lieutenant Noah Chamberlain. Who might you gentlemen be?"

"I'm Will Crockett. The big fella here is my little brother, Gid," Will said.

"Your little brother?" Chamberlain asked, noticing how big Gid was.

"He's younger than I am, and when we were kids, he was smaller. Somewhere over the last several years, he got a lot bigger, but he's still my little brother."

"You're with General Sterling Price?"

"In a manner of speaking. Our group just joined with him for this battle. We're with Quantrill."

Chamberlain gasped. "Quantrill?" After a moment's silence he continued. "Maybe you should leave me here," he suggested. "I think I can make it the rest of the way on my own."

"We'll take you a little closer," Gid said. "What's the matter. Does it bother you because we are with Quantrill?"

"Yes," Chamberlain admitted. "But I'm worried for you, not for me. You may not know this, but the orders are out. If any of Quantrill's men are captured..."

"We are not to be treated as prisoners of war, but as criminals," Will said. "Yes, we've seen the orders."

"But, don't you understand? If you are captured tonight, you'll be dead by sun up. They'll hang you."

"They haven't caught us yet," Gid said.

"Shh," Will whispered. "We're nearly to the Yankee lines. No sense in announcing our presence."

Will's warning was too late. From the darkness in front of them, two Yankee soldiers suddenly appeared. Both were carrying rifles, and they had the rifles in the ready position.

"Halt!" one of them called. "Who's there?"

"Yankee pickets," Gid said under his breath,

"Soldiers, I am Lieutenant Noah Chamberlain, of the Seventh Kansas," Chamberlain said.

The soldiers looked at Chamberlain. His blue uniform clearly announced who he was. Will and Gid were wearing gray.

"Who are these men? They look like Confederates," one of the pickets challenged.

"They are from General Price's staff," Chamberlain said quickly. "They have been guaranteed safe passage to bring me back to my own lines."

"I don't see no flag of truce or anything," one of the Yankee pickets said.

"They can scarcely show the flag while carrying me, can they?" Chamberlain challenged.

"No, sir, I don't reckon they can," the picket replied.

Chamberlain looked at Will and Gid. "Thank you very much for your help," Chamberlain said. "But I expect you two had better get back to General Price now, before your safe passage expires."

"I reckon so," Will said. "Good luck to you, sir."

When Chamberlain saw that one of the pickets was looking suspiciously at Will and Gid, he put his hand on the picket's shoulder.

"This is no place to stand around gabbing," Chamberlain said. "Why don't you two men help me back to the aid station? I have a mine ball in my leg, and it's going to have to come out."

"Yes, sir," the picket said.

With their attention diverted, Will and Gid were able to go back across no man's land.

"I'm sure glad that Yankee lied for us," Gid said. He put his finger in his collar, then pulled it away from his neck. "I wouldn't have taken too highly to hanging in the morning."

"Yes, but if anyone saw you hit a Confederate officer, our own people may hang us," Will said.

"You're right. I'm sorry I hit him."

Will looked at Gid in surprise. "You're sorry you hit him?"

"Yeah. I should've killed the son of a bitch."

"San Pedro! We're comin' into San Pedro, folks," the conductor called, walking quickly through the car. Will wasn't sure if he had been napping or just remembering, but at the conductor's call, he pushed his hat back and looked out the window as the train began creaking to a stop in the depot. Something outside the window caught his attention, and he sat up for a closer look.

"What the hell?" he said. "Gid?"

"Yeah, I see it," Gid replied, staring through the window at the same thing that had caught Will's eye.

A large cottonwood tree stood in an empty lot just east of the railroad depot. There, hanging from one of the high, straight limbs of the Cottonwood, was a corpse. The corpse's hands were tied behind its back and the head and neck were misshapen by the effect of the hanging. The corpse was twisting slowly at the end of the rope.

"Looks like there's a sign or something tacked onto his boot," Will said.

The two brothers got off, then walked up to the stock car to get their horses. The horses were a little skittish from the journey and had to be coaxed down the ramp.

When the horses were detrained, Will glanced again at the body that was hanging from the tree.

"Gid, you see anything odd about that?" Will asked, nodding toward the body.

"Odd?" Gid replied. "Hell no, what's odd about seeing a corpse hanging from a tree, right in the middle of town?" he teased.

"Yeah, well, that," Will said. "But the other thing is, there's nobody standing around looking at it. You'd think someone would be curious, wouldn't you?"

"You would think," Gid agreed.

"I am."

Gid chuckled. "I thought you might be."

"Let's go see what the sign says."

The two men led their horses into the empty lot, then stood under the tree and looked up at the man who was hanging there. Whoever hanged him had not put a hood over his face, thus leaving the grotesque visage of a violent death for all to see. The skin was chalky white, the cheeks were puffed, and the mouth was open. Flies were crawling in and out of the mouth. The worst part about him was his eyes. They were bulging nearly out of their sockets.

"Ever see him before?" Gid asked.

"No," Will said. "The way this fella is all puffed up though, I'm not sure I would recognize him even if I had seen him." Will pulled the sign off the corpse's boot.

"What does it say?" Gid asked.

" 'Stuart Oliver,' " Will read. " 'Leave him be. He'll hang here as a warning against all other cattle rustlers.' And it's signed by a fella named Stiles. Hmm, sounds like this fella Stiles doesn't much care for cattle rustlers," Will concluded.

"Well, whether Stiles likes cattle rustlers or not, I already don't like the son of a bitch," Gid said. He mounted his horse, then rode up close enough to be able to reach the rope. Taking out his pocket-knife, he cut the rope, and the body fell.

"What are you going to do with him?" Will asked.

"I don't know. Take him to the undertaker, I guess. There has to be one in town," Gid answered.

Looking around, Will saw a baggage cart by the edge of the depot. He brought the cart over, then he and Gid loaded the body onto it. Tossing a rope around the cart, the two brothers started riding toward town, pulling the cart with the body behind them.

Although there hadn't been anyone standing in the empty lot while the body was hanging, word quickly passed through the town that the body had been cut down, and as the two brothers pulled the cart down the street, a small crowd began to follow them. Most of the onlookers stayed to the side of the street, looking on in curiosity, but three men suddenly stepped out into the street in front of them. One of them was young, dressed in black. He had a silver band around his hat and his gunbelt was studded with silver conchos. Even his pistol was silver-plated and pearl-handled. He had an arrogant sneer on his face. The other two men hung back a step, deferring to the young, arrogant one.

"Get down off them horses," the arrogant one ordered.

Will and Gid looked at each other, then with a shrug, dismounted and stepped up toward the three men.

"What are you doin' with that?" the man in black asked.

Gid and Will looked toward the body, then back at the three men who challenged them.

"We found him," Gid replied.

"I know where you found 'im. What are you doing with him?"

"Well, I thought maybe we would take him to the undertaker's," Gid answered easily. "Maybe you can tell us where it is."

"Mister, maybe you didn't see the sign we left tacked to the son of a bitch's foot," the arrogant one said.

"Oh, you mean the one that said, 'Leave him be?' Yes, we saw it," Will said.

"Then you know we figured to leave this cattle thief

hanging for a while."

"That's not a good idea," Will replied as if discussing possibilities with them. "He's already beginning to get a little ripe. Besides which, it doesn't make a very good impression on anyone who might be coming in on the train, to see a corpse hanging there like that."

"That ain't none of your concern. Now, take 'im back, and hang him up where you found him."

"I can't," Will said. "He won't let me."

The leader of the group looked confused. "He won't let you? Who won't let you?"

"My little brother won't let me," Will said, nodding toward Gid. "He's got his heart set on seeing this fella get a proper burying. And as you can see, he's a pretty good-sized man. When he sets his heart on something, he pretty much gets his way."

As if unable to believe what he was hearing, the arrogant one looked at the two men with him.

"Did you hear what he said?"

"Yeah, Aubrey, we heard 'im," one of the two men said.

Aubrey stretched his face into what one might suppose was a smile, though it came out as little more than a grotesque sneer. "Looks like we're going to have three bodies hanging from the tree," he said. "The one we done hung, and these two we're about to shoot."

"Wait a minute. There's three of you and only two of

us. This isn't fair," Will complained.

Aubrey laughed. "Well, now, mister, life is like that sometimes."

"Yeah, I know," Will said, sighing. "It looks like I'm only going to get one of you. Gid will get the other two."

"What?"

"Which one do you want, Big Brother?" Gid asked, calmly.

"Well, since I'm only going to get one, I think I'd like to take this loudmouthed little son of a bitch they're callin' Aubrey," Will replied.

Aubrey turned to the others. "Will you listen to this? You'd think he .. .oof!"

That was as far as he got, because Will suddenly, and unexpectedly sent a vicious kick right between the man's legs, scoring a direct hit with the point of his boot. Grunting in surprise and pain, Aubrey doubled over, then went down. Will's sudden move had caught the others by such surprise that they looked at their fallen partner in shock.

Gid caught one of the remaining two men with a powerful roundhouse right to the chin. He went down and out like a light, alongside Aubrey, who was now lying in the dirt, moaning in pain.

By the time the third man realized he was the only one left, it was too late. Gid dropped him with a well-aimed punch as well.

The townspeople who had been following the boys from the moment Gid had cut the body down now cheered and crowded out into the street around them.

"Any of you know where we might find the undertaker?" Gid asked.

Two of the men pointed to a little building down the street, but neither of them spoke.

"Thanks," Gid said.

Chapter Four

Remounting, Will and Gid continued their ride down the middle of the street of San Pedro. Behind them, the steel-banded wheels of the little baggage cart they were pulling rang as they rolled across the hard-packed dirt. Farther behind still, the three men who had accosted them were just beginning to regain consciousness. Much of the town continued to follow, though they kept to either side of the street, maintaining what they figured would be a safe distance from Will and Gid.

Leaving the body with an undertaker who was somewhat less than enthusiastic over getting the business, the brothers' next stop was the nearest saloon. Again, they were followed by a score or more townspeople.

Gid laughed.

"What is it?" Will asked.

"So much for sneaking into the saloon and having a

quiet drink," he said.

"Don't know why that would bother you, Gid. I've never known you to do anything, quietly."

"You're the two gents who cut down Stuart Oliver, ain't you?" the bartender asked when they stepped up to the bar.

"I reckon that's us," Gid said.

"Then drink up, boys. The first one is on the house," he said. "What'll it be?"

Both boys ordered whiskey.

"Doesn't this town have any law?" Will asked, as he tossed the drink down.

"Yeah, we've got a town marshal," the bartender replied.

"Don't know what kind of marshal he is," Will said. "But I've not known many who just would stand by and watch a lynching."

"Oh, it wasn't a lynching," the bartender said. "Stuart was hung all legal and proper."

"You're sayin' that was a legal hangin'?" Gid asked.

"Yes, sir. There may be some don't agree with it. Fact is, I don't agree with it. Far as I know, Stuart Oliver was an all right kind of man. He come in here a lot.... was always quiet, and never give nobody any trouble."

"Then, how did he wind up trimming a tree?" Will asked.

"He went to Jackson and complained that some rustlers

was stealin' his cows."

"Jackson?"

"Simon Jackson. He's the marshal," the bartender said. "Anyhow, Jackson said he would look in to it, but the next thing you know, ole' Stuart was back in the marshal's office, claimin' that he just seen some of his cows bein' loaded onto the train cars. The marshal said he'd look into it, but Stuart didn't want to wait. Instead, he just went down to the pens, opened the gates, and started herdin' the cows off... big as you please, in front of God and ever'body. The cattle buyers swore out a complaint against him, and Stuart was tried for cattle rustling."

"You mean that's it? That's what they got him on?"

"Yes, sir. Well, they had him dead to rights," the bartender insisted. "I mean, the whole town seen him tryin' to take them cows."

"Seems to me like that would be more of a dispute over ownership than cattle rustling. And even if it was rustling, attempted cattle rustling is all they could really get him on," Gid said.

"Yes, sir, it does seem a shame. Like I said, Stuart was just general well-liked around town."

"But nobody came to his defense?"

"What could anybody do? I mean, it ain't like he didn't do it."

"What about the cattle he claimed were his? Anything

done about that?"

"By the time the trial come around, them buyers had already shipped the cows out."

Although Will was engaged in conversation with the bartender, he wasn't inattentive to what was going on behind him. In the mirror, he saw Aubrey come in. Aubrey made no attempt to approach them, but sat over in the corner instead, just watching.

"Do you know a man by the name of Chamberlain?" Will asked.

"Noah Chamberlain? Sure, everyone 'round here knows him. Is he a friend of yours?"

"An acquaintance," Will said. "I heard he's had some trouble with rustlers, also."

"I reckon he's had more trouble'n nearly anyone else. Some time back, three of his riders was found shot, and a lot of his cows was stole. Fact is, he had so many cows stole there's some folks bettin' he won't be able to make it much longer."

"Excuse me for interruptin' the conversation here, bar-keep," Gid said. "But who is that rat-faced bastard sitting in the corner over there? I heard the others call him Aubrey. Aubrey who?" Gid asked.

"His name is Aubrey Stiles. He's Doc Stiles's son."

"Stiles's son?" Gid said. "Well, no wonder he took an interest in leaving Oliver hanging from the tree. He was just lookin' out for papa's interest."

"Who were the two toadies with him?" Will asked.

"They're called Guy Townsen and Russ Bean. Anytime you see Aubrey, you'll see them two, suckin' up to 'im."

"Some folks are hard-pressed for friends, I reckon," Gid said.

"Tell me about the rustlers who stole Chamberlain's cows. They ever find them?" Will asked.

"No, sir. But the marshal's put up a pretty good reward for them. So has Doc Stiles."

"Stiles has put up a reward for the men who rustled Chamberlain's cattle? Why?" Will asked.

"Well, sir, the way Doc Stiles explains it, anyone who would rustle cows from one ranch, would rustle from any ranch. So he figures he's got as much at stake in getting' the rustlers caught as Chamberlain."

"Makes sense, I suppose," Will said.

The bartender nodded, then held up the bottle. "You boys want another drink?"

Gid leaned across the bar. "Your whiskey is good, bar-keep, but I was just wonderin' if maybe this town didn't have a few other things a man might need."

"I beg your pardon?"

"What my brother is talking about is women," Will explained. He looked around the saloon. "Come to think of it, I haven't seen any in here."

"Oh, there's a couple that hang around here, all right," he said. "But, by damn, they're so ugly they'd make a train take ten miles of dirt road. Now, if you really want to find some women, you might want to check out Big Sal's Place."

"Big Sal's Place? Is that another saloon?" Gid asked.

"Saloon, my eye. Big Sal's Place is a whorehouse, gents. A genuine, first-class whorehouse, run by a lady called Big Sal. Fact is, it's also a fine hotel with good rooms as well as a cafe. And anyone will tell you, they set the finest table in town."

"And where might this place be?" Gid asked.

"It's a big, fine-lookin' white buildin' at the far end of town on the other side of the street. You can't miss it."

"What do you say, Will?" Gid asked. "You want to check it out?"

"We may as well," Will replied. The bartender had been about to pour them another drink, and he was still holding the bottle. "Tell you what, friend," Will said. "How about selling me the rest of that bottle you're holding in your hand?"

"It's about half-full; give me a dollar and it's yours," the bartender replied.

Will paid him, then he and Gid turned away from the bar and stared at Aubrey Stiles. Aubrey, remembering his last encounter with them, grabbed his hat and hurried out of the saloon. By the time the boys stepped out onto the front porch, Aubrey was mounted and riding quickly out of town.

Big Sal's Place was made of wood, two stories high, with a second-story balcony that ran all the way around the building. Below the balcony, at street level, was a fine wooden porch with a dozen rocking chairs. A very large, heavily painted woman got up from one of the chairs and smiled a greeting at the two brothers as they dismounted out front. She was smoking a cigar, and as she approached them she tapped off the ash at the end.

"Greetin's, gents. My name is Salceda, but they call me Big Sal." Big Sal put her hand on a rather large hip, then gave it a bump, winking as she did so. "Don't have any idea why they call me that," she said.

Both boys laughed.

"You just visitin' the girls, or will you be takin' rooms?" Big Sal asked.

"Both," Gid answered.

"Well, if you're taking rooms, just leave your horses tied up there, and I'll have my man Harvey take care of 'em. We've got our own stables out back."

"That's nice," Gid said.

"Come on inside. I'll get you registered, and show you around."

The boys followed her through the double doors. For a

place in such a small town, the lobby seemed huge. There were a dozen or more chairs and sofas scattered about, several potted plants, mirrors on the walls, and a grand, elegant staircase rising to the second floor.

"Will you be wantin' one room, or two?" Big Sal asked.

"We spend enough time together," Will said. "Whenever we can, we always take our own rooms."

"And we'd like them on the front, if you don't mind," Gid added. "We like a view."

Big Sal studied the two men for a minute. "You boys on the dodge? I don't want any trouble here."

"We're not wanted," Will said.

"But you have been, haven't you? Else, you wouldn't insist on a room where you can keep an eye on the town."

"Old habits die hard," Will said.

"All right, gents," Big Sal said. She took two keys down from a row of nails and handed one to each of them. "Right at the top of the stairs, one on the left and one on the right."

"Thanks."

"You got a place to take a bath in this hotel?" Will asked, rubbing the stubble on his chin.

"Yes indeed," Big Sal said. She smiled proudly. "We even have a water tank on the roof so that we have running water."

While Big Sal was explaining how to get to the bathroom, Gid was looking around the lobby.

"Any more questions?" Big Sal asked.

"Yeah, where the hell are they?" Gid asked.

"I beg your pardon?"

"The girls? I thought this was a whorehouse."

"It is. There's not a better whorehouse within a hundred miles, if you ask me."

"Well?"

"Well, what?"

"Where are the whores?"

"Oh, I suspect most of them are sleeping. They work nights, you know."

"Can you roust one of them up?"

"Of course I can. Which one?"

"Well, since I don't know any of them, it makes no difference to me. Just choose one. Choose the one you like the best."

Big Sal laughed, a deep, throaty laugh. "Well, now, honey, I like men, not women ... so I don't have a favorite. But they are all fine-looking ladies, so I don't think you will be disappointed no matter who I select. I think I saw Annie up and about a few minutes ago. I'll send her to your room."

"Fine, fine," Gid said, rubbing his hands together in anticipation. He turned to Will. "Big Brother, it looks like you are going to have to do without my company for a while."

"I'll manage," Will said.

"Also, maybe you should let me take my bath first, so I won't stink too much for the lady."

Will chuckled. "I'm not sure you'll be able to get the stink off. But don't worry about me, I'll just take a look around and see what they have in this town."

Chapter Five

Fifteen minutes later Gid was in the bathroom, settled into the large brass bathtub. A clean shirt and clean pair of pants hung over the back of a nearby chair. On the floor beside him was half a glass of whiskey, and beside the glass, what was left of the bottle he and Will had bought. A cigar was elevated at a jaunty angle from his freshly shaved face, and Gid was trying to wash his back while at the same time singing, "The dew is on the grass, Lorena ..."

His singing was interrupted by the sudden and un-expected opening of the bathroom door. Grabbing his pistol, he brought it up, thumbing back on the hammer as he did so.

"Oh!" the intruder gasped, frightened by the pistol.

"You ought not to scare a fella like that," Gid said.

"I scared you? What do you think you did to me?" A very pretty young woman stepped into the room then, and closed the door behind her. She had dark hair, green eyes, and dimples.

"Uh, can I help you, miss?" Gid asked.

"No, but maybe I can help you. If you'll stop that infernal racket, I'll wash your back for you." She knelt down beside the tub, picked up the wash cloth, dipped it in the water, then started running it down his back. "I'm Annie Bowman. Big Sal said we should meet. What's your name?"

"Annie, is it? Well, Annie, my name is Gid Crockett. Are you telling me you don't care for my singing?"

"Is that what you call it, Gid? I've heard coyotes do better," Annie teased.

"Ah," Gid said in blissful appreciation. "A little more to the left. There, that's it. And, yes, I call it singing."

Gid sat silently for a minute as Annie soaped his back a second time, then washed it off again.

"Do you provide this kind of service for all your customers?"

"No," Annie said. "But I appreciate what you and your friend did for Mr. Oliver."

"Mr. Oliver?" Gid was confused for a moment. "Oh, you mean Stuart Oliver? The body we cut down?"

"Yes."

Gid sighed. "Don't think I'm not grateful for your appreciation, darlin', but cuttin' him down after he's already dead sure doesn't seem to me like we did much for him."

"Nevertheless, it was awful the way they let him just hang there. I could see him from the window in my room and I cried every time I looked."

"How well did you know him?"

"He was one of my regulars," Annie said without shame. She smiled at him. "Are we just going to talk all day? Or do you have something else in mind?"

Gid returned the smile. "As a matter of fact, I do have something else in mind," he said, "but I'll be damned if I'm going to do this in a bathtub. Let's go down to my room."

Gid strapped on his pistol belt and put on his hat. Then, unembarrassed by his nakedness, he and Annie walked down the hall, carrying his clothes and boots. Once in the room, he put his clothes down, then pulled her to him. He was surprised when she pulled away from him.

"What's wrong?" Gid asked.

"You aren't planning to be wearing that are you?" Annie asked with a giggle, pointing to the pistol belt.

"Uh, no, I guess not," he said. He unstrapped the belt, then hooked it over the bedstead, letting it hang in a way that would allow him quick access to the pistol.

"And that?" Annie said, pointing to the hat.

"What about you?" Gid said as he took off his hat. "You going to get out of your clothes?"

"I will now," she said, as with a smile she started to undress.

At one time, Marshal Simon Jackson had been a pretty good lawman. As a member of the St. Louis police department, he had been cited for finding, and bringing to justice the River Front Murderer. But that was fifteen years ago. Now, he was overage and overweight. He was the town marshal, not the county sheriff. That meant his authority extended only to the town limits, a fact he pointed out every time someone suggested he should go after Doran and his outlaws.

Jackson bemoaned the fact that he had no authority beyond the town limits, but in truth, he was glad he didn't have to be put to the test. He could still handle drunks and barroom fights. That was enough to satisfy both the mandate of his office and the dictates of his conscience.

Until the incident with Stuart Oliver, Jackson believed that he had enjoyed the support of most of the citizens of the county. And even the incident with Oliver could be justified. Oliver had clearly violated the law. He stole cattle from the loading pens. Nearly a dozen people in town saw him do it.

All Jackson did was arrest him. After that, the law took its course. Oliver was given a fair trial, found guilty, and sentenced to hang by the circuit judge. Everything was legal and above board.

It had been Stiles's idea to leave the body hanging as a warning against other cattle thieves. But even that violated no laws, though it did offend Jackson's sense of what was right and wrong. And, he told himself, maybe Stiles was right. Maybe it would serve as a warning to cattle thieves, though it seemed obvious to Jackson that Stuart Oliver's situation was different. He clearly wasn't one of the thieves who had been plaguing the county.

Jackson contemplated these things as he stood in his office.

He was drinking a cup of coffee and looking through the window, down Front Street.

Aubrey Stiles had come in earlier, protesting the fact that Will and Gid Crockett had attacked him, Townsen, and Bean, out in the street last night.

"From what I hear, you boys confronted them," Jackson said. "So, what do you want me to do about it? Arrest them for beating you up? I'll do it if you want me to, but folks are sure to get a laugh out of it."

"No. I can handle my own fights," Aubrey replied. "But somethin' ought to be done about them cuttin' Stuart Oliver's body down." Aubrey came over to stand beside Jackson. When he happened to look out the window, he saw Will walking up the sidewalk. "Hey, there's one of them now! Do you see him?"

"I see him," Jackson answered calmly.

"Well, what are you going to do about it?"

"What do you propose that I do about it?" Jackson asked, turning toward Aubrey. "All they did was cut down a body that had been hanging from a tree for two days. That's not breaking any law that I know of."

"Ain't you got no paper on them? I heard people talking about them. Their name is Crockett, Will and Gid Crockett. They rode with Quantrill during the war. I heard near 'bout all them is wanted men now."

"That may be true, but they aren't wanted in my town," Jackson said.

"Damn! He's comin' in here!" Aubrey said, realizing then that Will was headed straight for the marshal's office. Aubrey looked around quickly. "I... I'd better scoot out the back. It wouldn't look good for him to see us together."

"You can go down the alley," Jackson said. He watched, barely able to contain a smile, as Aubrey sneaked out of the back door.

The front door opened a moment later and Will Crockett stepped inside.

"You the marshal, or the deputy?" Will asked.

"I'm Marshal Jackson, Mr. Crockett. I don't have a deputy. The town budget doesn't allow for one. What can I do for you?"

It didn't surprise Will that the marshal knew who he was. On the contrary, he would have been surprised if the Marshal hadn't known. With the reputation he and his brother had developed, he had grown to expect to be known by the lawman of just about every town they visited.

"Where can I find Doc Stiles?" Will asked

"What do you want with him?" he asked.

"He's the biggest cattleman around here, isn't he?"

"That's right."

"Then I need to talk to him."

"You sure you want to do that? Cuttin' ole Stuart Oliver down from that tree like you and your brother done won't sit none too well with Doc Stiles. Not only that, you beat up his son."

"That's true, but I still want to talk to him."

"Are you the law?" Jackson asked.

"In a manner of speaking."

"What do you mean, in a manner of speaking?"

"There is a reward being offered for bringing in the rustlers that killed Chamberlain's men, isn't there?"

"Yes."

"Then, in a manner of speaking, anyone who goes out after that reward is working for the law."

Jackson studied Will through squinted eyes. "I never would have believed this," he said. "Are you telling me you and your brother are bounty hunters?"

"It's not what I would call our profession. But we are

going after the rustlers who killed Chamberlain's men."

"You and your brother are welcome to try, of course, but I'm afraid you will find that it's not all that simple. People around here have been looking for Rollo Doran and his bunch for nearly two years now. What makes you think you can find 'em, when no one else has been able to?"

"Because we generally do what we set out to do," Will answered. "Now, where is Stiles?"

"His ranch starts about five miles north of here. You can't miss it. Once you get there, it stretches for as far as you can see in any direction."

"Thanks," Will said, starting toward the door.

"Crockett?" Jackson called.

"Yes?" Will turned back toward the Marshal.

"Outside the town limits, you and your brother can poke around all you want. But when you are in town, don't forget who the real law is around here."

"Well, now, seems to me like that's the question, isn't it?" Will replied. "Just who is the real law around here?"

"By god, I am," Jackson said, in a blustering answer.

"Is that a fact? Does Stiles know that?" Will asked.

Chapter Six

One of the amenities the customers could enjoy at Big Sal's was a friendly game of cards. On the wall there was a sign which read: This is an honest gambling establishment. Please report any cheating to the management.

In addition to the self-righteous claim of gambling integrity, the walls were also decorated with game-heads and pictures, including one of a reclining nude woman. Some marksman had already added his own improvement to the painting by putting three holes through the woman in all the appropriate places, though one shot had missed the target, slightly, giving her left breast two nipples. There was no gilt-edged mirror, but there was an ample supply of decent whiskey, and several large jars of pickled eggs and sausages placed in convenient locations.

By the time Will returned to Big Sal's Place, all the girls were up and tending to business. Will saw one of the girls taking a cowboy up the stairs with her.

The upstairs area didn't extend all the way to the front of the building. The main room, or salon, was big, with exposed rafters below the high, peaked ceiling. The "grand" salon, as Big Sal insisted upon calling it, was almost like a private club. There were a score or more customers present, sitting on the sofa or in big easy chairs, talking with the girls, drinking, or playing cards.

Big Sal came over to Will, then put her arm through his.

"Welcome back, Mr. Crockett," she said. "I trust you had a productive day as you wandered around our little town."

"It was all right," Will said. He looked around the salon. "Where's my brother?"

Big Sal laughed. "Let's just say that your brother's day has been equally productive, though perhaps in a different arena. Could I get you something to drink, Mr. Crockett?"

"Yes," Will said.

"Wine, beer, or whiskey?"

"Whiskey," Will said.

"Edie, do keep Mr. Crockett company while I get him something to drink," Big Sal said, adroitly putting Will with one of her girls. Edie was heavily painted and showed the dissipation of her profession. There was no humor or life left to her eyes, and when Will didn't appear to show too much interest in her, she turned and walked over to sit by the piano player.

The piano player wore a small, round derby hat and kept his sleeves up with garter belts. He was pounding out a rendition of "Buffalo Gals," though the music was practically lost amidst the noise of a dozen or more conversations.

"Oh, my, you didn't like Edie?" Big Sal asked, returning with Will's whiskey.

"Edie was fine," Will said. He put his arm around as much of Big Sal as he could. "But after being greeted by you, everyone else seems second rate."

Big Sal laughed out loud. "My, my, Mr. Crockett, you do have a golden tongue," she said. "But you'd better be careful who you flirt with. I might decide you're serious. Oh, excuse me, some more customers just came in."

Big Sal left Will standing alone in the middle of the salon, smiling and drinking his whiskey.

One of the customers, a young cowboy, got up and walked over to Will, carrying his beer with him.

"Hello, Will. I heard you and Gid were in town."

"Leigh Burleson, isn't it?" Will asked. "Last time I saw you was in San Angelo, I believe."

"You've got a good memory," Burleson said.

"Still trying to fill an inside straight?" Will asked, recalling a card game they once played.

"Haven't had any more luck with that here than I did

back there," Leigh answered with a chuckle.

"What are you doing in these parts?" Will asked.

"Trying to make a dollar. I've hired on with Mr. Chamberlain."

Will took a drink, studying Burleson over the rim of the glass. "Is that a fact? I heard Chamberlain had a little trouble there a while ago."

"You got that right. Three of our men were killed, and a couple hundred head of cows were stolen."

"You have any idea of who did it?" Will asked.

"Hell yes, I know who did it. Everyone knows who did it."

"Rollo Doran?" Will asked.

"You know about him?"

"I've heard the name, that's all."

"Doran and a band of outlaws have a hideout somewhere in the hills nearby. Nobody's been able to find out just where. Or, if anyone has, they've not lived to tell about it. What brings you and Gid to town?"

"A man's got to be somewhere," Will replied.

"I hear you might be going after Doran, for the bounty."

"Where'd you hear that?"

"I was talking to Marshal Jackson."

"Well, if a bounty falls in our lap, we won't walk away from it," Will replied.

"If you're goin' to get involved, I think you should

know that we practically have a range war going on between the rustlers and the ranchers. You could be bitin' off more'n you bargained for."

"Wouldn't be the first time we wandered into a hornets' nest," Will said.

Leigh nodded. "Yeah," he said. "Well, I didn't figure you'd just pull up stakes and go away. But don't say you wasn't warned."

"Will, open the door," Gid called the next morning. Will opened his eyes and looked around. A bright morning sun was streaming in through the open window. He heard Gid call out again, this time augmenting his call, by banging on the door.

"Will, you awake in there?"

"Yeah," Will said. He got out of bed, yawned and stretched, then padded over to the door in his bare feet and opened it. He stepped back to let his brother in.

"You tryin' to wake the dead?" Will complained.

"You plannin' on sleepin' all day?" Gid countered, barging into the room. He walked over to the window and put it all the way up. "You need some air in here. No wonder you were still asleep. It's stuffy."

"What time is it?"

"Damn near six-thirty," Gid replied. "Half the day is gone already."

"Oh, well, hell, what was I thinking, laying up 'til near noon like that?" Will replied sarcastically. He went over to the basin and began brushing his teeth. He had no toothpaste, so he used whiskey.

"I love the smell when the morning sun hits the fresh piles of horse shit in the street, don't you?" Gid asked. He took a deep breath.

Will chuckled. "You're crazy, Little Brother, you know that?" he said. "And I don't know where you get it from, 'cause I know it didn't run in the family."

Gid turned away from the window. "Will, didn't you say you wanted to ride out to Stiles Ranch today?" Gid asked.

"Yeah, I thought it might be time we meet this fella face-to-face."

"There's no need to go out to his ranch to do that."

"What do you mean?"

"He's coming to a meeting of the Cattlemen's Association."

Will began working up a shaving lather. "Maybe we ought to try and get ourselves an invite to the meeting," he suggested.

"We've already been invited. By Noah Chamberlain."

"You've been to see Chamberlain?"

"Didn't have to go see him. He's downstairs right now," Gid said. "Waiting to have breakfast with us, in fact."

Chamberlain was in the salon having coffee with Big Sal when Will and Gid came down the stairs. He stood to greet them.

"When Leigh Burleson told me you two men were here, I didn't believe him," he said. "But here you are, in the flesh. It's good to see you boys." He smiled at Will. "Still carrying water to your wounded enemies?"

"Not so much, these days," Will said. "It's become more difficult to find honorable enemies."

"Isn't that the damned truth?" Chamberlain agreed.

"Gentlemen, I've set a table, just for you," Big Sal said. "This way."

Big Sal led them, not into the main dining room, but to a smaller, much more elegant, and more private room. A breakfast buffet was laid out for them, and the men moved through slowly, filling their plates.

"What brings you boys to San Pedro?" Chamberlain asked.

"You," Will said.

Chamberlain looked at him in surprise.

"Me? How so?"

"Or rather, what happened on your ranch a month or so ago."

"You mean about my three riders getting killed? Yes, that was really a shame. Look here, Will, did you know any of them?"

"No. I heard about Archie Walters from his sister, Dora," Will said. "She tried to hire Gid and me to look into it."

"How is Dora getting along?"

"She seems to be doing just fine."

"After Archie was killed, I tried to get Dora to move over here," Chamberlain said. "I told her I could get her fixed up with Big Sal. But, she's got friends over there. And she said she didn't want to have anything to do with a town that could let an innocent boy like her brother get killed, and do nothing about it." Chamberlain looked across the table at Will. "You say she tried to hire you? No need of her spendin' her money to find out who killed my men. Tell me what she offered, and I'll pay it."

"I told her we didn't want her money," Will said.

"Too bad you aren't interested."

"I didn't say we weren't interested," Will said. "I just said I didn't want to take her money. From what I hear, there is already a reward posted."

"There is, but rewards are pretty iffy things. On the other hand, I have a proposal that might interest you. How would you like to work for the Cattlemen's Association? I'm sure they would be willing to compensate you generously."

"Gid told me you had invited us to attend the meeting today. Will Doc Stiles be there?" Will asked.

"Stiles? Yes, he'll be there. He's president of the association. I'm the vice-president."

"Stiles might not be in a hiring mood," Gid suggested. "Particularly as we cut down his tree decoration."

Chamberlain chuckled. "You let me handle Stiles. He's frustrated, like all the rest of us. I'm telling you, Doran and his rustlers are worse than a plague of locusts. He's already run a couple of good ranchers out of business, and he's hurt us all, Stiles included."

"All right, Mr. Chamberlain," Will said. "We'll apply for the job."

With Chamberlain as their sponsor, Will and Gid were invited into the inner sanctum of the Cattlemen's Association. Some of the men, Will noticed, had been at Big Sal's Place the night before, and though they nodded at each other in recognition of the fact that they had seen each other there, no one spoke of it.

As Chamberlain had promised, Doc Stiles was present for the meeting. He was a fairly small man, with curly gray hair, dark, beady eyes, a narrow mouth, and a nose which was shaped somewhat like a hawk's beak.

In addition to Chamberlain and Stiles, there were four other men present. They were dressed as businessmen, but Will saw immediately that they would have been much more comfortable dressed exactly as he and

Gid were. The ranchers were used to the saddle and to range clothes, and they pulled at their collars and tugged at their sleeves.

Doc Stiles was more formally dressed than any of the other ranchers, wearing a three-piece suit and a silk shirt, with a diamond stick-pin in his tie. As the wealthiest man in the territory, Doc Stiles was a natural for the position of president of the San Pedro Cattleman's Association.

Other men might have felt intimidated by this display of ostentation, but Will and Gid were neither impressed nor intimidated. Instead, they sat there listening to Noah Chamberlain as he made his pitch to the board.

"I think I can speak for all the cattlemen when I say that we have come to the conclusion that desperate measures are needed to stop the terrible plague of rustling we have been experiencing," Chamberlain said.

"I'll say. If this goes on any longer, it's going to drive me out of business," one of the other ranchers said. He was a big man with a sweeping moustache.

"Yeah, and not only Kimball here, but me and Holeman and Ashby too," another added.

"Do you want the floor, Mr. Woods?" Stiles asked the one who was speaking.

"Well, yeah, I guess. I mean, hell, I thought I already had the floor," Woods replied.

"You don't have the floor until the chair says you have the floor," Stiles explained. He cleared his throat, then made a show of announcing: "The chair now recognizes Emmett Woods." Stiles looked at the others. "Let's keep this in order. If we are going to spend money to hire a couple of men, then everything has to be above board. All right, Emmett, you may speak."

'Thanks," Woods said. "I guess we all know that Doc Stiles is about the only one stout enough to keep going. In fact when the rustlers hit me really hard a couple months ago, it was Doc Stiles that loaned me the money I needed to make a note at the bank. If it wasn't for him I don't know what I would do."

"At least you're tryin'," Holeman said. "Maxwell and Logan just chucked it in and went back home."

Doc Stiles leaned back in his chair and sighed. "I'm afraid the truth is they were too small to even try it out here. Of course, their instinct was to fight back, but when the rustlers started hitting them, they didn't have anything to fight with. They weren't left with enough cattle to even make all the ends meet, and they went under."

"It could've been worse," Woods said.

"How could it have been worse?" Holeman asked. "Neither one of them is here anymore."

"It could've been worse because they might have had

to go back East with nothing. As it is, they at least had enough money to get them back."

"Yeah, you're right. Thanks to Doc Stiles buyin' 'em out, they didn't leave here completely broke," Holeman agreed.

"You mean you have their ranches now?" Will asked, raising his eyebrows.

"Yes."

"I see."

"No, Mr. Crockett, I don't think you do see," Woods interjected. "Doc Stiles didn't have to buy them out. Hell, once they abandoned their ranches the land was out there, just for the taking. Doc Stiles paid them for it when, by law, he didn't have to pay them a cent."

"I couldn't just take over," Doc Stiles said. "I wouldn't have felt good about that. After all, both men did have families to support."

"He's made the same standing offer to the rest of us," Woods said. "And I have to confess that knowing he will buy us out if need be gives us a little more incentive to try and get something done."

"It could also make you less willing to stand and fight, figuring you can always sell out and leave," Gid suggested.

"Yeah, well, I'm not ready to leave just yet," the rancher named Kimball said. "So, I'm willin' to see what it is you boys can offer us."

Kimball took two cigars from his jacket pocket and gave one to Will and the other to Gid. They accepted, and after biting off the ends, waited for Kimball to provide the match. Kimball lit both of them and they were able to take several puffs before Stiles spoke up.

"I understand you two boys had a run-in with my son last night," he finally said.

"We had a little difference of opinion on that cottonwood tree that stands down there, next to the depot. Aubrey and his friends thought it should be decorated. My brother and I thought it shouldn't."

Doc Stiles chuckled. "I'll say this for you two boys. You settled it pretty fast. They tell me you rode with Quantrill."

"Yes, during the border war between Missouri and Kansas."

"Is that what it was? A border war?" Stiles asked.

Will took a puff of his cigar, then, with squinted eyes, stared through the smoke at Stiles. "Yes," he finally said after a pause that was so long that the others were beginning to think he wasn't going to speak at all. "It was a border war."

"But you did ride with Quantrill?"

"We did."

"So they rode with Quantrill. What's your point, Stiles?" Chamberlain finally asked.

"It's funny that you, of all people, would have to ask

66

me that, Chamberlain," Stiles replied. "You were an of-ficer in the Union Army, weren't you? You know what kind of men Quantrill's riders were. Besides, why am I having to explain this to you, or to anyone?"

"I know what kind of man Quantrill was," Chamber-lain said. He nodded toward Will and Gid. "But I also know what kind of man each of these men were. They conducted themselves with honor then, and I see no reason to think otherwise of them now."

"Yes, well, it's not just their wartime experiences that I'm talking about," Stiles said. He looked at Will and Gid. "I have heard of your exploits since the war's end. In fact, a lot of people have. You two have the reputation of leaving a lot of dead men in your wake."

"We've left our share of dead," Will admitted. "But we've never killed unless it was a time for killing."

"I see," Stiles said. "And, who decides when it is a time for killing."

"We decide when it's time for killing," Gid said. Gid's words fell upon the room with the impact of pistol shots.

"Hell, that's fine with me," Woods suddenly said. "Truth is, we want you two to hunt the rustlers down. We want you to hunt them down and when you find them, we want you to kill them on the spot."

Will took the cigar out of his mouth and studied the end of it for a moment before he looked up at Woods.

"It's like my brother said, Mr. Woods. We are the ones who will decide when it's time for killing," Will said. "But we don't kill on command, and we're not professional executioners."

Woods raised his eyebrows. "You're squeamish about killing?"

"Not at all. As I said, we have killed when it was necessary. But unnecessary killing is a waste of time and energy."

"If you ask me, it's bringing these sons of bitches in to be tried that is a waste of time and energy," Holeman said. "Why don't you just kill 'em, and be done with it?"

Will stood up and put his cigar down on the ashtray.

"You gents don't want us. You want a couple of assassins. You can get someone else."

Doc Stiles began clapping his hands slowly, as if applauding a performance.

"Bravo," he said. "Bravo, Mr. Crockett." Doc Stiles smiled at the other members of the organization. "Gentlemen, if I had any doubts about these men before, I have none now."

"What is this?" Will asked.

"Well, my dear fellow, when I agreed with these gentlemen to discuss hiring outside help, I had certain reservations. I wasn't sure just how far you would go. I was concerned that if we gave you carte blanche you might unleash a bloodbath in our fair valley." He smiled at Will and Gid. "But, after listening to you talk, I now believe that you are men of integrity and ethics. Most of all, you are men with a sense of values. I can, in all good conscience, employ your services, and know that there will not be a sudden onslaught of wanton killing. Gentlemen, you are hired."

"We're not hired, unless we say we are hired," Will said. He picked the cigar up again. "Now, we have a few questions of our own, if you don't mind."

"But of course you do," Doc Stiles said. "I imagine the first thing you want to know is what will be your pay?"

"That's a start," Will said.

"Yes. Well, I propose that we pay you two hundred fifty dollars per month, plus a bonus of two hundred fifty dollars for every cattle thief you eliminate by, uh, whatever method is needed, regardless of the reward that is currently in effect. In addition, you will receive whatever government award is in effect, whether more or less. And when you bring in their leader, Rollo Doran, we will pay you one thousand dollars. Not only that, you can begin drawing your money immediately. We are prepared to give you a two-hundred-fifty-dollar advance."

"The money sounds reasonable enough," Will agreed.

"You will, of course, be required to report in to us often," Woods said. "We want to know what's going on."

"No, we won't do that," Will said.

"Why not?" Kimball asked.

"You ever heard the story of putting a bell on a cat?" Will asked. "If we have to report in here to you people, the outlaws will always have an idea of where we are."

"But look here! This is ridiculous," Woods sputtered. "We can't be expected to pay you two this kind of money and then have absolutely no idea as to where you are, no control over where you go or what you do."

"That's the way it's going to be," Will said.

"Of course it is," Noah Chamberlain said. He looked at the others. "Listen to me, gentlemen. I say we need these two men. And if the only way we can employ them is to hire them on their own terms, then I don't see that we have any choice but to comply."

There was grumbling exchange of conversation for a moment or two, then Kimball spoke up.

"All right," he said. "If Noah here is satisfied with them, then I am too."

Kimball's acquiescence brought on agreement from all the others, including Doc Stiles, who then renewed the negotiations.

"You can operate any way you want, come and go as you like. The only thing we want is for these damn rustlers to be eliminated. Because if they aren't wiped out, and wiped out fast, there may not be any cattlemen left in this entire valley."

Will relit his cigar, smiled at them, then he and Gid started for the door.

"Wait!" Stiles called. "Are you going to take the job?"

Without looking around, Will held his cigar up and nodded.

"When will we hear from you again?"

"When we come for our money," Will replied.

Chapter Seven

It had been three days since Will and Gid agreed to take the job, and two nights since several cows were stolen from Holeman's herd. Last night the rustlers hit again, taking cows from Woods's ranch.

Angered, Woods called a meeting at his house of all the ranchers in the valley.

As the nearby mountains turned from red to purple in the setting sun, Woods's friends and neighbors began arriving for the meeting. Wagons and buggies brought entire families across the range to gather at the Woods house. Children who lived too far apart to play with each other laughed and squealed and ran from wagon to wagon to greet their friends before dashing off to a twilight game of kick-the-can. The women, who had brought cakes and pies from home, gathered in the kitchen to make coffee, thus turning the business meeting into a great social event. Many of them brought quilts and they spread them out so that, while the men were meeting, they could work on the elaborate colors and patterns of the quilts they would be displaying at the next fair.

The cowboys were invited too. They had an interest in the proceedings, for if the ranchers lost their ranches, the cowboys would lose their jobs. However, the cowboys were working hands and they didn't feel comfortable around the ranchers and their families, so most of them declined, respectfully.

Doc Stiles attended the meeting, accompanied by his son, Aubrey. Aubrey went straight to the sideboard for a glass of whiskey.

Chamberlain was the last rancher to show up. He came in a buckboard, accompanied by his wife, Elsie, and his daughter, Dottie. Dottie was, according to all the cowboys, by far the prettiest young woman on the range. Aubrey had made a few overtures toward Dottie and many believed they would eventually wind up together.

"No way a pretty woman like that is going to marry a no-count like Aubrey Stiles," some of the more adamant of the cowboys protested. "There's no way she could love him."

"Love has nothing to do with it," the more pragmatic of the cowboys pointed out. "Besides, Doc Stiles is all right. Aubrey's just spoiled, that's all. He's spoiled 'cause he grew up rich. But he'll come around."

When Chamberlain arrived, Aubrey was standing on the porch. He hurried out to offer his assistance to Dottie as she stepped down from the buckboard. She smiled at him, being very careful to make the smile one of courtesy, and not invitation. Once inside, Dottie hurried back to the kitchen to join the women.

"Let's get the meetin' goin'," Woods suggested.

The Chamberlain Ranch was three miles south of the Woods ranch, where the meeting was being held. Because Chamberlain had not yet replaced the three men who had been killed, there were only four cowboys still working at his place, and, they, like the cowboys from all the other ranches, had been invited to the meeting. But also, like many of the cowboys from the other ranches, they had declined.

The ranch cook had made the meeting, in fact he had gone over earlier to help prepare a meal for all the attendees. That left the four cowboys to shift for themselves, and one of them, Paul, was cooking supper for the other four.

"You think all them ranchers is goin' to come up with anythin' at this meetin' they got goin' on over to the Woods place?" Shorty asked, as the four of them sat around the supper table.

"I don't know. If they don't, they're all goin' to go out

of business and me an' you an' Curly an' Paul is all goin' to be lookin' for jobs somewhere else."

"Maybe we could wind up workin' for Doc Stiles," Shorty suggested. "Seem's like ever'time someone quits ranchin', he takes over."

"Yeah, but if you notice, he don't hire all the cowboys from the old ranch. Hell, he don't even hire half of 'em. The rest of 'em is left out in the cold," Curly said.

"Yeah, that's true," Shorty agreed.

"What I'm hopin' is that them two fellas they hired will stop the rustlin'," Leigh went on.

"I don't know. That seems like a pretty big job for just two men," Paul said.

"The Crocketts aren't just ordinary men. I know, because I've run across them before."

Leigh looked over at the man who was cooking their supper. He smiled, and waved his hand in the front of his nose. "What the hell is that you're cookin' over there, any-how, Paul? Some dead skunk you found out on the trail?"

"Listen, you don't want to eat it, you can always rustle up your own supper," Paul replied, stirring the pot.

"Hell, I didn't say I wasn't goin' to eat it," Leigh an-swered. "I just said it stinks, that's all."

"Leigh, you're as full of shit as a Christmas goose," Shorty said. "Don't pay no never mind to him, Paul. You know him. He'd eat the north end of a southbound mule while the mule was still walkin'."

Outside the bunkhouse, six riders stopped on a little hill overlooking the ranch and ground-tied their mounts. They crept to the edge of the hill, crouched down, then looked down toward the bunkhouse.

"Looks like they's four of them here," one of the men said. "I can see 'em through the window. Three of 'em's sittin' at a table and another one is standin' up."

"Don't matter how many is here. Doran said kill 'em all, so let's commence shootin'. You three, aim at the one that's sittin' on the left and the one standin'. Me and Jake and Dirk will take the other two."

"I'm ready," Jake replied.

All four men raised their rifles and took slow, careful aim. Their targets were well illuminated by the lantern that burned brightly inside the bunkhouse.

"Shoot!" the little group's leader said, squeezing the trigger that sent out the first bullet.

Suddenly Paul, who was standing at the stove, let out a little grunt of pain, spun around once, then fell to the floor.

"What the hell you doin'?" Shorty asked, laughing at what he thought was a joke.

"Boys, I been shot!" Paul gasped.

The laughter died in Shorty's throat as bullets began crashing through the glass windows and popping through the thin board walls, smashing crockery, careening off the iron stove, and projecting lead splinters and shards of glass like miniature bursts of shrapnel.

"My God! My God! What is it? What's happening?" Curly shouted.

"Get down!" Leigh shouted. He dropped to the floor and crawled over to the window while bullets continued to crash and whiz through the little shack. When he looked out the window, he saw three men with rifles hiding behind the watering trough, firing at the bunkhouse. There were another three over behind the stable fence.

"Rustlers!" Leigh yelled, but there was no one left to hear him. When he looked back inside, he saw that the other three were already dead.

Leigh knew he had to get out of there, or he would be dead, too. The walls of the bunkhouse were too thin to stop the bullets. The only protection they could offer would be to mask Leigh's movement. Using that to his advantage, Leigh managed to tear out a couple of floor boards. As soon as the hole was big enough, he crawled through it to the ground below the cabin.

He felt the dank coolness of the dirt, smelled its odor, and breathed a small prayer of thanks that he had come this far without being hit. Whoever was shooting at the cabin did not realize that Leigh had slipped away, for the bullets continued to crash through the cabin overhead with the intensity of a heavy hail.

Lifting up his head just enough to see where he was going, Leigh slithered on his belly to the back of the bunkhouse, then rolled down into a small depression that allowed him to move, undetected, several feet away. Here, he was able to let himself down into a gully that was deep enough for him to stand. Once there, he started running without looking back, until the gunfire behind him sounded no more ominous than corn popping on a stove.

Will and Gid were camping at least two miles away from the ranch when they heard the shooting. Because of the echo, however, they couldn't be sure of the direction the shooting was coming from. Will climbed to the top of a large rock outcropping while the firing was still going on to see if he could find out. Then, far to the west, he saw a series of winking lights and knew that they were muzzle flashes.

"It's Chamberlain's place," Will said.

Gid was already extinguishing the camp fire. Will jumped down from the rock and within a couple of minutes both horses were saddled and the camp was broken.

Back at the meeting at the Woods Ranch, the ranchers were complaining bitterly over the fact that rustling was still going on.

"It's time we did something about it," Holeman said.

"We did do something about it. We hired the Crockett brothers," Chamberlain replied.

"The Crocketts ain't done shit."

"Give 'em time."

Woods held up his hands to quiet the group, then he nodded toward Doc Stiles, who had been watching and listening to the whole thing. So far, Doc Stiles had said nothing.

"I think maybe Doc Stiles might have a suggestion or two for us," Woods said.

At Woods's invitation, Stiles stood up to address the other men who were gathered there.

"Gentlemen, what we need," he began, "is to form a corporation. A cattle corporation."

"What do you mean?" Holeman asked.

"Yeah, how would something like that work?"

"It's really very simple," Doc Stiles explained. "We would merge all of our ranches and our cattle into one large cattle company. We would each own a share of the company, in proportion with what we put into it."

"What would be the advantage of such a thing?" Chamberlain wanted to know.

Stiles started to answer, then he saw the wood box sitting by the stove. Though the stove was cool now, the wood box was full, including the smaller sticks used for kindling. Stiles reached down and picked up a few of them.

"When you're gatherin' sticks for a fire," Stiles said, "have you ever noticed how easy it is to break one stick?" He snapped a single twig. "But put several of them together and you can't break them, no matter how hard you try." He demonstrated his point by putting several of the sticks together.

"That works with sticks," Chamberlain said. 'But I need a more practical answer."

"All right, how about this for an answer?" Stiles went on. "Suppose you put five-hundred head into the corporation and say, two hundred and fifty head were stolen. You wouldn't, personally, be out two hundred and fifty head. You would be out only a portion of that two hundred and fifty head, because the rest of us would absorb the loss with you."

"If they are his cows, why should the rest of us lose anything?" Ashby asked.

'Because, we'd all be partners in this thing," Stiles answered. "We would share in each other's adversity and in each other's success. We would be like brothers."

"That sounds pretty good," Holeman agreed. "If you put it that way, then I'm for it."

"Yeah, me too," Ashby added.

"Well, it looks like it's up to you, Chamberlain. What do you say?" Woods asked.

"I don't know," Chamberlain replied. "It might be hard, going it alone. But I'm not ready to give up my own ranch and start riding for Doc Stiles."

"It wouldn't be that way," Stiles said. "You won't be working for me. You'll be like all the other owners, a partner in a ranch that is bigger than anything you've ever dreamed of."

"What about the men we'd need to work an outfit this large?" Chamberlain asked. "Who would they be workin' for? Me, or this big ranch? I've only got four hands left, and I sort of hate losing control over them."

"They'd still be your men."

"You say that. But when it comes right down to it, somebody's goin' to have to be the boss, right?" Chamberlain asked.

"Yes, of course," Doc Stiles replied. "You would have anarchy otherwise. We could make the election of a president our first priority."

"I agree," Holeman said. "I say we elect the president now. Anyone got any ideas who it should be?"

"I say we elect Doc Stiles," Woods proposed.

"I second that," Ashby said.

"He's got my vote," Holeman put in.

"Chamberlain, it's up to you, now," Woods said.

"I'd like some time to think about it."

"Time? Man, we're runnin' out of time! The rustlers is bleedin' us white!" Woods said.

Suddenly someone burst through the front door, startling everyone with his unexpected entrance. His clothes were dirty and torn. His face was scratched by brush, his hat was gone, and he was bent over with his hands on his knees, breathing hard.

"Mr. Chamberlain! Mr. Chamberlain!" he shouted. "You gotta come quick!"

"Leigh, what is it?" Chamberlain asked, recognizing that this apparition was actually Leigh Burleson.

"The ranch has been hit! Curly, Paul, an' Shorty have been shot dead!"

"What?" several men gasped.

"And the ranch has been set afire."

"Leigh's right, Mr. Chamberlain, I can see the fire from here," one of the others called back into the house from the front porch.

Chamberlain and the others ran out onto the front porch. They could see the distant flames licking up into the night sky.

For a moment, everyone just stood there, mesmerized by the scene. Then, Holeman called them into action. "Well, come on!" he shouted. "If we get over there in time, we might be able to save some of it!"

"I've got extra buckets in the barn!" Woods said. "Get 'em in the wagons men, an' let's go!"

"What's the point?" Aubrey asked. "By the time we get there, it'll be too late."

"You're not going with us?" Doc Stiles asked his son.

"There's enough of you. You don't need me," Aubrey said. He took a bottle of whiskey from the sideboard, and tucked it under his arm. "I reckon I'll just get on back and keep an eye on our place. You never can tell where they might hit next."

Chapter Eight

It was quiet where Will and Gid waited in the rocks. They could hear crickets and frogs, a distant coyote and a closer owl, but nothing else. They strained their ears in vain for the muffled sounds of approaching men, the drum of horses' hooves, the rattle of the saddle and tack.

"Maybe they won't come this way," Will suggested.

"They'll come this way," Gid insisted. "It's the only way they can come, without running into the others."

"Shh, wait! There they are!" Will whispered. He had just gotten a glimpse of five men, silhouetted against the orange glow of the burning ranch. For a moment it was as if the gates of hell had opened, allowing five of its most desperate tenants to escape.

Will pulled his pistol and checked his load. Gid did the same.

The riders continued their ghostly approach, men and

animals moving as softly and quietly as drifting smoke.
Will cocked his pistol and raised it.

"Hold it right there!" he called.

"What the hell?" one of the men shouted. "Who is it?"

"Shoot 'im down!" another called.

The riders pulled their pistols then and opened fire.
The night was brightly lit with the muzzle flashes and
streaks of flame as Will, Gid, and the five mounted men
exchanged gunfire. One of the men dropped from his
saddle and skidded across hard ground. Flashes of orange
light exploded like fireballs on the rocks.

Will and Gid were well positioned in the rocks to
pick out their targets. The outlaws, on the other hand,
were astride horses that were rearing and twisting
about nervously as flying lead whistled through the
air and whined off stone.

Gid picked out one of the riders and tumbled him
from the saddle.

"Where the hell are they?" one of the two remaining
outlaws shouted in panic.

"Let's get out of here!" the other yelled.

They didn't make it.

Then it was quiet, with the final round of shooting
but faint echoes bounding off distant hills. A little cloud
of acrid-bitter gun smoke drifted up over the deadly
battlefield and Will and Gid walked out among the fallen

rustlers, moving cautiously, their pistols at the ready.

It wasn't necessary. All five men were dead, and the entire battle had taken less than a minute.

Half a mile back down the trail, Vic Armstrong saw and heard the battle. His horse had picked up a rock and that delay caused him to fall behind the others. It also saved his life.

In the east, the sun was a full disk above the horizon. A dozen wagons were parked in the soft morning light, and in the wagons, nestled among the quilts and blankets, slept the children of the families who had come to help fight the fire. The morning light now disclosed the damage done. The main house and bunkhouse had been completely destroyed, but it could have been worse. Had Chamberlain not taken his wife and daughter with him to the meeting, they might now be lying dead in the smoldering ruins. The smoke house, granary, and barn had not burned because they were protected from the flames by the prodigious efforts of those who had come to fight the fire.

Elsie Chamberlain stood in her husband's arms, weeping softly. Dottie stood close to her parents, looking at the destruction with eyes that were wide and sad. The Chamberlains, like everyone else out there, were covered with ash and soot from the blackened ruins of their home.

On the ground under a tree, sat a pitiful pile of what few belongings they had managed to pull from the ashes. Most of their belongings were burned and twisted beyond recognition, but here and there a few things had survived the flames and their bright, undamaged colors shined incongruously from the pile of smoking, blackened rubble. The cast-iron cook stove stood undamaged, almost defiantly, in the midst of what had been the kitchen.

Everyone was tired and filled with a great sadness for the three young cowboys who had been killed. In addition to their deaths, the death of a home was also particularly hard, because this was an area where homes and people were few and far between.

"How many were there?" Jackson asked Leigh. This was the first chance he had had for interrogation, because the entire night had been passed in the effort to protect the other buildings.

"I'm not sure," Leigh replied. "Four, five, six. I was too busy dodging bullets to count."

"Did you recognize any of them?"

Leigh, who had helped fight the fire, was black with soot and ash. He walked over to the well and brought up a bucket of water, then took a long drink from the dipper, not yet having answered the marshal's question. He wiped the back of his hand across his mouth, leaving a clean swipe through the soot.

"Well?" Jackson asked again, impatient with Leigh's stalling.

"I'm not real sure," Leigh finally said. "Like I said, I was busy dodging bullets. And besides that, it was dark. But when they set fire to the main house, it lit up the yard some, and that's when I got a pretty good look at one of them. I wouldn't swear to it, you understand, but I'm pretty sure I recognized a couple of 'em."

"Who were they?" Stiles asked, coming over to join the conversation and showing, by his question, that he was as eager as the marshal to find the guilty party.

"Vic Armstrong was one of 'em."

"Vic Armstrong. It figures," Jackson said. "He's one of Doran's men, all right."

"The thing is, I'm sure I saw Jake Simmons with 'em too."

"Jake Simmons? Are you sure?" Jackson asked, his face plainly showing that the information was difficult for him to accept.

"Well, like I said, I don't know if I could swear to it," Leigh hedged. "But it sure looked like him."

Jackson looked over at Doc Stiles. "Simmons works for you, don't he, Stiles?"

"He did work for me," Doc Stiles agreed. "But he doesn't anymore. He took his pay and rode on about a month ago. I'd be surprised if he fell in with Doran, though. I'm sure you're mistaken, Leigh."

"I could be," Leigh admitted. "But it sure looked like him."

"There's someone comin' in!" Woods called, and the men who had fought the fire all night long now stirred themselves to meet the riders.

"There's two of 'em, leadin' a string of horses," one of the others said. "What is it, a pack train?"

"No, look. Look what's on the horses. It's bodies."

There were gasps of shock and surprise from all present, and they hurried out to meet the riders as they approached.

"It's the Crocketts," Holeman said.

As Will and Gid rode into the front yard of what had been Chamberlain's house, they saw the men and women gathering together to meet them. Will signaled Gid, then they stopped near one of the wagons. Will climbed down from his horse and, taking his canteen from the pommel, walked over to the well to fill it. All eyes were on him, not only the men, but the women and children as well. The men crowded down close, the women hung back, and the children were back, farther, in some cases hiding behind their mothers' skirts, peering out around them with wide, curious, and in some cases, frightened, eyes.

"Crockett, you want to tell us what all this is about?" Doc Stiles asked.

As Will poured water into his canteen he looked around at the smoking ruins of what had been the house.

"Doesn't seem like you should have to ask," he said.

"See here, Crockett, are you saying these men did this?" Jackson asked.

"That's what I'm saying."

"How do you know they did it?" Woods asked.

Will put the top on his canteen and hooked it over the pommel.

"There's five of them. I believe our deal was, two-hundred fifty dollars each," Will said.

"You haven't answered my question, Crockett," Woods said. "How do you know these are the men who did it, unless you saw them do it? And if you saw them, why didn't you stop them then?"

Jackson had walked over to the six horses and was checking each of the men by grabbing a handful of hair and lifting the head.

"I'll be damned, Leigh. You were right. This one is Jake Simmons," he said.

Leigh went over to Simmons's body and grabbed a handful of hair. He lifted the head and stared into the face. Simmons's eyes were open, but they were opaque with a death stare. Leigh looked up at Gid, who was still sitting quietly on his horse.

"I just wish it had been me instead of one of you that

90

shot 'em. They killed Shorty, Curly, and Paul."

"It doesn't really matter who killed him, does it?" Gid asked. "He's just as dead."

"Yeah," Leigh said. He let the head fall back down, then brushed his hands together. "Yeah, I reckon the son of a bitch is, at that."

"All right, boys, if you two will come into town tomorrow, I'll have a bank draft for twelve hundred fifty dollars drawn in your favor," Stiles offered.

Will nodded, then remounted his horse. "We'll see you tomorrow," he said. Touching his hat as if in greeting to the ladies, he and Gid rode away from the Chamberlain Ranch, leaving behind the gruesome cargo they had brought in.

It was late that afternoon when Vic Armstrong approached the entrance to a canyon that was about ten miles northwest of the Chamberlain Ranch. The canyon was known as Hidden Canyon, for the simple reason that it was so well concealed by the rocks and ridge lines which guarded its entrance that it couldn't be seen unless someone was specifically looking for it. At the entrance to the canyon there were two tall natural obelisks from which someone could keep a watchful eye, thus preventing anyone from approaching the canyon without being seen. Down inside the canyon there was a source of water.

For these virtues Rollo Doran had selected Hidden Canyon as his hideout. There were half a dozen adobe shacks to house the rustlers, as well as the handful of women, most of whom were burned-out soiled doves, who had joined the group.

As Armstrong approached the canyon entrance, he stopped and removed his hat, then waved it broadly across the top of his head, put it back on, then took it off and waved it a second time. This was the prescribed signal, and only then did he see the series of mirror flashes which told him he could enter.

Doran was told that a rider was coming in, so he came outside his cabin to wait. Doran, a short but powerfully built man, suffered from some rare affliction that made him almost completely hairless; he was not only bald, but lacked eyebrows and beard as well. As a result, his head looked somewhat like a cannonball. He had been eating when he heard that someone was coming, so he wrapped a tortilla around some beans and took it outside with him. Some of the juice dribbled down his chin but he made no effort to wipe it off.

"It's Armstrong," someone said.

"Armstrong? Alone?"

"Yeah."

"I wonder what happened to the others?"

The rustlers and the women who had made the canyon

their home knew that six riders had gone out yesterday. They were curious as to why only one was returning, and they drew close to see what Armstrong would have to say. The women of the camp hung back, out of the way of the men, but still close enough to hear the news. One of the women was an olive-skinned, black-eyed senorita named Bella. Though no one but her closest friend knew it, she was carrying Jake Simmons's child. She hadn't even told Jake yet, because she was afraid he would leave if he knew.

"What happened?" Doran asked.

"You ain't goin' to like it," Armstrong said.

"Tell me anyway."

"It's about the Crockett brothers," Armstrong said. "You know that the Cattlemen's Association hired them."

"Yeah, I heard about 'em."

"Well, they was waitin' for us. They threw down on us from the rocks, had three killed 'fore we even knew we was in danger. I managed to fight my way out," Armstrong lied, "but none of the others was that lucky. The Crocketts killed 'em all."

"Jake's dead?" Bella asked with a gasp.

"Jake Simmons? Yeah, he was the first one to be killed," Armstrong said coldly.

"Oh, Jake!" Bella wailed, and she wandered away crying, comforted by one of the others.

"What about Chamberlain's ranch?" Doran asked.

"Did you get the job done?"

Armstrong smiled. "Yeah. We killed all his hands, and burned his house and bunkhouse," he said, smiling proudly.

"Good job! Good job!" Doran said happily. He smiled in triumph. "With most all his hands dead, that means Chamberlain's cows are there for the takin'. I reckon we'll pay 'em a visit tonight."

It was late in the afternoon of the day after the fire. The neighbors who had gathered to fight the fire were all gone now. Only Chamberlain, his wife and daughter, and Leigh, remained behind to see to the cleanup. A wagon, its wood bleached white by the sun, sat a few feet in front of the blackened remains of the house, as it was being filled with the ashes and burned boards to be hauled away. All four were working when Dottie saw two riders approaching.

"Pa, Ma, here comes two men," she called to the others.

"Who is it?" Chamberlain asked.

Looking up, Leigh shielded his eyes against the sun. "It's the Crocketts, Mr. Chamberlain," he said.

"I wonder what they want?" Elsie said. "They frighten me."

"You've got no reason to be frightened of them," Chamberlain said.

"I know. You've told me the story of how they saved

your life during the war. And I know they're on our side. But I've heard so much about them. They are violent men," Elsie said, with a shudder.

"It is a violent world," Chamberlain replied. "Sometimes you need a little violence on your side." He started toward the riders. "Howdy, Will, Gid. What can I do for you boys?" he asked.

Both Will and Gid dismounted. Will handed the reins of his horse to Gid, who then led both animals over to the watering trough to let them drink.

"Mr. Chamberlain, how many head of cattle do you have?" Will asked.

"About twenty-five hundred or so," Chamberlain answered. "Why do you ask?"

"Because, unless I miss my guess, Rollo Doran will be coming after them soon."

"By soon, you mean when?"

"Tonight."

"Oh," Elsie gasped.

Chamberlain patted his wife's hand reassuringly, then looked at Leigh.

"Leigh, I figure you got wages comin'," he said. "I'm goin' to pay you off now so you can get out of here."

"Are you firin' me, Mr. Chamberlain?" Leigh asked.

"No, not exactly. You can come back tomorrow... if I have any cows left. You'll still have your job if you want it. But I don't figure this is your fight, so I want you to take Elsie and Dottie on into town."

"What do you mean, take me into town?" Elsie asked. "I'm staying out here. You can't fight them off by yourself," she protested.

"He won't be by himself, Mrs. Chamberlain," Will said. "My brother and I will be here with him."

"You? Why would you do such a thing?" Chamberlain asked. "It isn't your fight."

"Oh but it is. The Cattlemen's Association is paying us to make it our fight, remember? We'll be right here when they come."

"I will too," Leigh said.

"Leigh, you sure you want to do this?" Chamberlain asked.

"I'm sure. I figure I owe 'em for Paul, Shorty and Curly," Leigh said. "Besides that, I put too much work in these cows just to see someone ride in and take 'em away."

Chamberlain smiled. "Well, that's the mark of a good foreman, I reckon."

"Foreman?" Leigh smiled broadly. "Look here, Mr. Chamberlain, are you tellin' me you're makin' me the foreman of this ranch?"

Chamberlain laughed. "I reckon I am," he said. "Seeing as how you're the only hand I got left. But if we don't keep Doran from takin' all our cows tonight, there won't be no ranch to be foreman of."

"We'll stop him, Mr. Chamberlain," Leigh said. "You just tell me what you want me to do.'

Chamberlain looked at Will and Gid. "Well, I reckon that's up to these boys. Have either of you got any ideas?"

"Yeah, a few," Will admitted

"Can they wait until after we've had a meal?" Elsie asked. "It's gettin' on toward suppertime. I thought I'd fix us somethin' to eat."

"Thank you, but we've got some jerky in our saddle bags," Will said.

Gid got a pained expression on his face. "Hold it, what are you doing turning down a meal?" he asked.

Will pointed to the burned-out house. "I figure these folks got enough to deal with, without having to worry about cooking a meal."

"Nonsense," Elsie said. "The rest of us have to eat, don't we? What's two more mouths to feed? Anyway, the stove is still here and I've just about got it cleaned up and ready to use. And the smokehouse is still full of meat. If we're going to fight a war tonight, we're goin' to do it on a full stomach."

"Mrs. Chamberlain, you're a lady after my own heart," Gid said. He looked at Will, pleadingly. "What do you say, Will?"

Will smiled, and nodded. "All right," he said. "I guess

there's no arguing with you when you're hungry." He looked at Elsie. "If you are certain it won't put you out any."

Elsie laughed. "Mr. Crockett... the house has been burned down around us. Would you please tell me how in the Sam Hill I could be put out any more than I already am?"

Will chuckled. "No ma'am, I don't guess I can tell you."

"Come on, Dottie. Help me feed these hungry men."

Chapter Nine

Gid found a place under a tree. Will was sitting on an overturned bucket, eating a supper of pork chops, fried potatoes and scrambled eggs. Chamberlain, who had just finished his own supper, came over to talk to him.

"You been givin' some thought to what we might do tonight?" he asked. "I mean, do you have any ideas on how we can stop Doran?"

"I have been givin' it some thought," Will said. He put down his plate, then stood up and pointed to the open end of the valley. "Anyone who comes in is going to have to come that way, unless they come over the mountains."

"That's right," Chamberlain agreed. He chuckled. "And even if they could get in that way, they couldn't get nothin' back out unless they were stealin' mountain goats."

"All we need to do is pick us out a few good places and wait. Once they come in, we'll open up on them.

Only thing is... we should get into place before it gets dark so we all know where everyone else is. That way we'll know not to shoot each other."

"Will, suppose we light a lantern and hang it in the granary?" Gid suggested.

"Why would you want to do that?" Chamberlain asked. "Seems to me like that would just draw 'em in."

Will and Gid looked at Chamberlain and smiled. Then, Chamberlain nodded. "I see what you mean," he said. "We'll be usin' the lantern as bait."

"I'll hang the lantern," Elsie offered.

"Good," Will answered. He pointed to the barn. "I'll be up in the loft with a rifle. Gid?"

"Yeah?"

"You think you can get up onto the smokehouse without eating everything that's in it?"

Gid laughed. "I reckon I could, if I took a pork chop or two to gnaw on," he teased.

"Mr. Chamberlain, you and Leigh set up behind these two water troughs," Will said. "The water will help stop the bullets."

"Till it all leaks out," Chamberlain said with a chuckle.

"Well, if we haven't run 'em off by the time all the water can leak through a couple of bullet holes, we'll prob'ly be dead, anyway," Leigh suggested.

"Oh!" Elsie gasped.

Realizing what he had said, Leigh apologized quickly. "Miz Chamberlain, don't pay no attention to that," Leigh said. "I was just funnin', that's all."

"You have a most unusual sense of humor, Mr. Burleson," Elsie said.

"Yes'm, I reckon I do. I apologize about that."

"No apology needed, Mr. Burleson."

"What about me?" Dottie asked Will. "Where do you want me to go?"

"I want you and your mother to get down into the root cellar and stay there," Will ordered.

"What do you mean? You aren't keeping me out of this," Dottie complained.

"Dottie, do what Mr. Crockett says."

"But Pa, you know I can shoot as well as most men."

"I know you can, honey, when you're shooting at tin cans, or bottles and the like," Chamberlain said. "But this is for real, and I don't aim to take any chances with you or your mother."

Dottie pouted, but said nothing else.

"Well," Will said, walking over to his horse and pulling a rifle out of the saddle holster. He took a box of shells from the saddlebag. "I guess we'd better get to it while it's still light."

Everyone started moving into their own positions. Dottie, who was still pouting, didn't move.

"Dottie, go on now," Chamberlain scolded gently.

With one more defiant look, Dottie turned and walked toward her mother, who was now washing the dishes in a bucket of water.

With his rifle in hand, Will climbed up into the hayloft over the barn, then started looking toward the west, toward the open end of the draw, from which direction Doran and his men would be coming.

From this vantage point, Will could see why Chamberlain had chosen this particular setting to build his house. He was treated to one of the vistas he had come to greatly appreciate during his years of wandering through the West. The setting sun, losing both heat and brilliance, but none of its vibrant orange color, seemed poised in the west above the desert floor. A dark gray haze was beginning to gather in the notches of the rugged escarpment, hanging there like drifting smoke. The red sandy loam was dotted with blue cedar and mesquite, limned in gold from the setting sun.

"It's beautiful, isn't it?" a woman's voice said.

Startled, Will turned to see Dottie just coming off the ladder, onto the loft. She was carrying a rifle.

"What are you doing here?" Will asked harshly.

"This is my home, Mr. Crockett," Dottie said. "Or at least, what is left of it," she added. "I don't care what you or Pa say, I don't intend to sit on my hands while someone tries to take it away from us."

"This is no place for a woman," Will insisted.

Dottie held up her rifle. "The bullet that comes out of here doesn't know whether it's been shot by a man or a woman," she said. "I'm staying, and there's nothing you can do about it, unless you plan to throw me out of here physically."

Will stroked his chin for a moment as he stared at her. She was right, there wasn't anything he could do about it. And, if she had that much gumption, maybe she would be useful.

"All right," he agreed, reluctantly. "You can stay."

"Ha," Dottie said with a snort. "As if I needed your permission."

Despite himself, Will laughed.

Will looked around to find the others. He saw Gid lying on his stomach on top of the smokehouse. Leigh was kneeling behind one of the watering troughs, peering intently over the top. Chamberlain was lying on his stomach, peering around the edge of the other watering trough.

"Looks like everyone is where they're supposed to be," Will said quietly. "Everyone except you." He turned toward her and saw that she had been staring at him.

"Mr. Crockett," she started.

"Call me Will."

"Will. Do you think I'm pretty?" Dottie asked.

Will chuckled.

"What is it? Why are you laughing?" Dottie asked sharply.

"Here we are, waiting for a shooting war to begin with who knows how many rustlers, and you want to know if I think you're pretty."

"Well, am I?"

Will looked at her. She was flirting openly with him now. Sometimes, innocent young women tended to do that. He never really knew whether they were attracted to him out of gratitude when he helped them, or out of a sense of excitement from the danger he represented to them. Whatever the reason, he didn't like to encourage it. He had a thousand reasons why such a thing shouldn't be encouraged, none of which he was willing to share because the very act of sharing why he couldn't be interested could, in itself, be mistakenly construed as an act of encouragement. If he needed a woman there was always Big Sal's Place, or a soiled dove in the next town. He neither needed, nor wanted, any involvement with some fresh-scrubbed rancher's daughter.

"Miss Chamberlain, when this is all over, I'll be drifting on," Will said quietly.

Dottie looked down at the toe of her boot. She knew he had read her mind and she knew he was telling her now that she was barking up the wrong tree. And yet, she couldn't bring herself to turn away from him. She had to try one more time to see if there was something, down inside the man, she could appeal to.

"You know, Will," she said, pawing at the barn loft self-consciously with her foot. "There's a lot of good grazing land in this valley, more than enough to support two or three families. If you were ever interested in, well, maybe in starting your own ranch, you could do worse than to do it here."

"I'm sure I could," Will said. He looked at her for a moment, then his voice softened. "Dottie, I can't settle down here. I can't settle down anywhere. If I did, I would get homesick."

Dottie was clearly confused. "Homesick? How could you be homesick? I thought you didn't live anywhere."

Will chuckled. "I don't," he said. "And that's what I would get homesick for. That's the worst kind of homesick you can have."

"I... I understand," Dottie said.

"I hope you do," Will said quietly. "You're as fine a young woman as I've ever run across, and you deserve a fine man. I'm not that man."

"I guess I made a fool out of myself," Dottie said. "I'm sorry."

Will smiled at her. "I expect in a few days I'll probably

look back on this and figure I was the one who made a fool of himself," he said. He looked out toward the gathering dusk. "Can you really shoot, Dottie Chamberlain?"

Dottie laughed. "I can snuff a candle at a hundred yards. Is that good enough shooting for you?"

"Good enough," Will agreed. He pointed over to the corner of the barn. "You get over there," he said. "The wall is double-planked there, and the vent-hole is big enough for you to poke your rifle through."

"Not much for picking out targets though," Dottie complained.

Despite himself, Will chuckled. "You'd complain if you were hung with a new rope," he said. "You're up here, aren't you? If I had my way, you'd be back in the root cellar. Now, get over there like I said."

Dottie smiled. "Yes, sir," she said. "Whatever you say, sir." She saluted.

Once Dottie got into position, Will stepped back up to the door and resumed his watch. It was dark and quiet. Over by the granary, the lantern burned brightly. A coyote howled and an owl hooted.

———

There was the scratch of hooves on the ground and the creak of riders in saddle leather. Rollo Doran twisted in his saddle and stared down toward the ranch. The house

106

and bunkhouse were gone, but there was a single lantern burning in one of the remaining outbuildings. It seemed incredible to him that they had managed to sneak up on Chamberlain's ranch without being seen, but that was just what had happened.

"Watch out!" someone said in a short, angry voice.

"Keep it quiet," Doran hissed. "You want them to hear us?"

"Hell, what if they do? Who's here? One man, his wife and daughter? All the ranch hands are dead."

"Nevertheless, keep quiet," Doran said. "No sense in lettin' 'em know we're here."

"They're goin' to find out pretty soon," one of the men said. He laughed a short, evil laugh. "Especially the girl. I aim to make a special point to let her know I'm here."

"Only if you beat me to her," one of the others added, and they all laughed.

"I wouldn't be worryin' none about the girl," Doran said. "When I give the word, I want ever'one to shoot toward that lantern. Like as not they're all inside there, and, small as it is, if we shoot it up good we'll prob'ly get all of 'em. But, don't shoot until we get closer and I give the word."

"Right," one of his men agreed.

Will saw them coming, and, though it was now too dark to signal his brother, he knew that Gid had seen them too. He knew, also, that Gid knew enough not to shoot until they were close enough for the first shot to be effective.

"Will!" Dottie hissed. "They're comin'!"

"Yes, I know," Will called back, quietly. "Dottie, don't shoot until I shoot."

"All right," Dottie replied.

Will raised his rifle and waited. They were still too far away and it was too dark to make them out well enough for a shot, or even to determine exactly how many there were. Then, finally, they drew close enough. He saw them raise their rifles and aim at the lantern in the granary. Gid's trick was working.

"Fire!" one of the riders barked.

With the muzzle flash from their rifles, Will had a target. He squeezed off a round, firing just to the right and slightly below one of the muzzle flashes. He heard a grunt of pain.

"What the hell? Where did that come from?"

Will's firing was a signal for the others to open fire as well, and Gid, Chamberlain, and Leigh began shooting.

"What the hell? They been waitin' for us with a whole army!" one of the attackers shouted in a frightened voice.

"We got to get the hell out of here!"

Will heard the sound of hoofbeats as the night-riders turned their horses and began beating a retreat. The defenders fired three or four more times but they were just shooting in the dark with no idea as to where their targets were. It didn't really matter. The idea now was simply to run them off, and that they did.

Will shouted down to the others. "All right! Hold your fire! Save your ammunition! They're gone!"

Will and Dottie climbed down from the hayloft, then joined Gid, who jumped down from the top of the smokehouse.

"Anyone get hit?" Will asked.

"No, but I think we hit a few of those bastards!" Leigh said, still excited, flushed with victory over their successful skirmish.

"We did it!" Chamberlain said. "By golly, we ran them off! They won't be back!"

"Not tonight," Will agreed. "And maybe not to your ranch at all, but most of 'em got away and if they don't come here, they'll try somewhere else."

"There's at least three of 'em won't try anywhere else," Gid said somberly.

"Three of them," Will said. "Those three are yours, Mr. Chamberlain. At two hundred fifty dollars each, that's seven hundred and fifty dollars. You think you could rebuild your ranch house with seven hundred and fifty dollars?"

"Oh, no, I couldn't," Chamberlain said.

"Sure you can," Gid said, seconding his brother's offer.

"I just wouldn't feel right trafficking in another man's death," Chamberlain said.

"Noah Chamberlain, don't be a fool," Elsie said determinedly, coming out of the root cellar then, to join them. "You and Leigh and Dottie helped kill those men."

"Dottie? What do you mean, Dottie helped?"

"She ran out of the root cellar before it all started," Elsie said. "I thought she came to join you."

"No, I didn't know anything about it," Chamberlain said.

"I was in the barn, Pa. With Mr. Crockett."

Chamberlain looked at Will. "I hope she didn't get in your way," he said.

"Not at all. She handled herself very well," Will said.

"But about your offer ..."

"Noah, if these men are generous enough to make this offer, I don't intend to let you refuse. If you won't take the bodies into town and claim the reward for them, I will."

Chamberlain sighed, then looked at Will and Gid. "I thank you boys," he said.

Will nodded, then looked over at Gid. "I reckon we'd

better be going," he said.

"Where are you going?" Dottie asked.

"Out there," Will answered without elaboration.

"But, where will you be if we need you? If this happens again?"

"We'll be around," Gid replied.

Chapter Ten

In less than two days the valley had been turned into a battlefield. The Cattlemen's Association had now paid bounty on eight rustlers. Rustlers or not, the sudden demise of eight young men quickly became the subject of every conversation in every bar in town.

"The Crocketts got them first five, you'll remember, then when that bunch hit Chamberlain's place why, he 'n Leigh got three more," one man explained.

"I heard that the Crocketts got 'em, too, but they just give 'em to Chamberlain to give him enough money to rebuild his house."

Aubrey Stiles listened to the babble of conversation. He was a listener, rather than participant, because even though conversations were going on all around him, he wasn't included. It wasn't an effort in concert by the others to exclude him. It was just that Aubrey was known as an arrogant young man with a quick temper. The best way to avoid any trouble with him, was to avoid, as much as possible, any contact with him.

Thus it was that, while social discourse went on at a fevered pitch all about him, Aubrey sat at a table with Guy Townsen and Russ Bean. Aubrey was playing a game of Ole' Sol, though he would have preferred a game of poker. Unfortunately, neither Townsen nor Bean had enough money to play cards, and no one else would play with him, because they didn't want to risk getting him angry.

Aubrey was not someone a person wanted to get angry. He was very good with his guns, and most believed that he looked, openly, for opportunities to use them. Last year, over in Cochise Springs, he killed a man in a poker game after the man accused him of cheating. Of course Aubrey had been cheating, but he couldn't let the accusation go unchallenged. The other man drew first, so there were no charges filed against Aubrey, even though he had goaded the other man into drawing.

The story was that Aubrey had also killed a man over in Benson for somewhat the same reason, but no one was really sure about that. That was because Aubrey hadn't given that man a chance to draw. Instead, he had waited outside the saloon, and when the man came out some time later, Aubrey shot him down from ambush. Though neither of the two men Aubrey had killed were known to be gunfighters they were, nevertheless, victims, and victims were all he needed to enhance his reputation as a man to be avoided.

Aubrey counted out three cards but couldn't find a play. The second card of the three was a black seven. There would have been a play had it come up on top. Unfortunately, it was one card down and therefore useless to him. Aubrey glared at it for a moment, then, with a shrug, played it anyway.

The bat-wing doors swung open and a cowboy came in and walked over to the bar. He was a working cowhand, not a gunman, and Aubrey recognized him as someone who rode for Holeman, though Aubrey didn't know the cowboy's name. The cowboy ordered a whiskey, then looked around and saw Aubrey sitting at the table, calmly playing cards.

"I just been thinkin' about Curly, Paul, and Shorty," the cowboy said to no one in particular. "They was good hands, cowmen who never did no harm to nobody. And they was shot down in cold blood."

Though the cowboy wasn't telling the people in the saloon anything they didn't already know, no one responded to his outburst. He had obviously been drinking before he came here and now he was in an expansive and dangerous mood.

"They was shot down in cold blood and the Chamberlain Ranch, where they worked, was burned out," the cowboy went on. "But then, you was all out there helpin' to fight the fire ... you all seen it," he said. He looked around the room, then his eyes fell on Aubrey who was still, pointedly, dealing and studying his cards. "That is, ever'one who was out there helpin' put out the fire seen it.

"But you wasn't there, was you, Aubrey Stiles? You and them two egg-sucking mongrels you got hanging around you all the time," he added with a derisive slur toward Townsen and Bean. "Tell us how is it that you three wasn't out there to help fight the fire at the Chamberlain Ranch, like the rest of us."

Aubrey looked up nonchalantly. "You talkin' to me, cowboy?"

"Am I talkin' to you?" the cowboy repeated. "Hell yes I'm talkin' to you, you low-assed, card-cheatin' son of a bitch."

The others in the saloon gasped at the cowboy's careless choice of words. Aubrey, however, just smiled coldly.

"Hey, do you know who you're talkin' to?" Townsen started, but Aubrey put his hand out to quiet him.

"It's all right, Guy," he said. "The cowboy is just drunk, that's all. I'm inclined to let that remark pass."

"You're a lucky man," Townsen said. "Aubrey wouldn't let somethin' like that pass with most men."

"I don't want him to let it pass. I asked how come it

is, that you three wasn't out to help fight the fire at the Chamberlain Ranch with the rest of us?"

"Why should I be out there?" Aubrey replied. "I've got my own ranch to run." He rifled through the cards as he talked, and found another play on the table.

"What do you mean, you've got a ranch to run? You got nothin' to say 'bout what goes on out at the Stiles spread. Hell, ever'body knows you don't even take a piss, 'lessen your pa tells you you can."

Aubrey looked up from the cards again. This time the nonchalance was gone. Instead, his eyes were narrowed menacingly. "Cowboy, I don't believe I know your name," he said.

"My name is Palmer. Earl Palmer. Not that it makes any difference to you."

"Oh, that's where you're wrong. It does make a difference to me, Palmer. You see, me an' you are about to have us a fight."

Palmer grinned broadly. "A fight? Yeah," he said, "that would be jake by me. Let's see, there's three of you and one of me, but I don't figure those two pissants you have with you got enough gumption to join in." Palmer made his hands into fists then held them out in front of his face, moving his right hand in tiny circles. "Come on," he said. "I'm goin' to enjoy this."

"I'm afraid not, Mr. Palmer," Aubrey said. "That isn't

the kind of fight I'm talkin' about. I plan to make this permanent."

Palmer lowered his fists slightly, staring at Aubrey with a confused expression on his face. "What do you mean, make it permanent?"

"We'll fight with guns, not with fists."

Palmer croaked what might have been laughter. "Yeah, you yellow-bellied bastard. I figured you might want to try something like that. That's why I ain't carryin' no gun with me. No, sir. We're goin' to settle this like men. We won't be using guns."

"Oh, but we will," Aubrey said. "Everyone in here heard you challenge me."

"No, they heard me call you a low-assed, card-cheatin' son of a bitch," Palmer said, grinning broadly. He still wasn't aware of the extent of his danger. "You the one that challenged me." He began making tiny circles with his right fist. "So, come on, let's get on with it."

"Yes, let's do," Aubrey said. He stood up and stepped away from the table, letting his arm hang down alongside his pistol as he looked at the cowboy through cold, ruthless eyes. "I'll let you draw first."

"I told you, I ain't drawin' on you," Palmer repeated. "No, come on over here and take your beatin' like a man."

"I said draw," Aubrey repeated in a cold, flat voice.

The others in the saloon knew, well before Palmer,

that the cowboy had carried things too far. There was going to be gunplay and they began, quietly but deliberately, to get out of the way of any flying lead.

It wasn't until that moment, seeing the others move out of the way, that Palmer began to worry that he might actually be losing control of the situation. He was still holding his fists in front of him, and he lowered them, then stared at Aubrey incredulously. "Are you deaf, Stiles? Ain't you been hearin' me tell you that I'm not wearin' a gun? If you're figurin' on forcin' me into a fight, you can just figure again, 'cause I ain't goin' to do it."

"I'll give you time to get yourself heeled," Aubrey offered.

"I told you, I ain't goin' to get in no gunfight with you."

"If you aren't goin' to fight, then get out of here. Get out of this saloon, out of this town, and out of this valley. Leave with your tail tucked between your legs, like the cowardly mongrel you are."

"No, I ain't doin' that, neither," Palmer said. "I got a right to live where I want and to say what I want." He picked up his drink, hoping by that action to show his defiance. What he showed instead was his fear, for his hand was shaking so badly that some of the whiskey sloshed over.

"You got no rights that I don't let you have," Aubrey growled. "Now, you walk through that door right now, or pull a gun."

"I told you, I'm not packin' a gun."

"Somebody give him one," Aubrey said coldly. He pulled his lips into a sinister smile. "Mr. Palmer seems to have come to this fight unprepared."

"I don't want a gun," Palmer said.

When no one offered Palmer their gun, Aubrey pointed to another cowboy who was standing at the far end of the bar. This man was carrying a pistol.

"Give him your gun," Aubrey ordered. "You aren't going to be using it."

"He don't want a gun," the man said.

"Oh, I think he does."

"Listen, Aubrey, you don't want to pay Palmer any mind. He was good friends with them boys that was killed out at Chamberlain's place and he's just upset, that's all. Why don't you just leave it be?"

"I said give him your gun."

"I ain't goin' to do that. If I give him a gun, you'll kill him."

"That's right."

"Well, then I don't want no part of it."

"You have no choice, my friend. You'll either give him your gun so I can kill him, or keep it for yourself, and I'll kill you," Aubrey said. He turned three-quarters of the way toward the armed cowboy. "Which will it be?"

"Now, hold it! This ain't my fight!" the cowboy said,

holding out his hands, as if by that action he could stop Aubrey from doing anything.

"Give him your gun, or use it yourself," Aubrey said again.

The cowboy paused for just a moment longer, then sighed in defeat. "All right, all right. If you put it that way, I reckon I'll do whatever you want." He took his gun out of the holster and lay it on the bar. "Sorry, Earl," he said. He gave the gun a shove and it slid half-way down the bar, smashing through two glasses, then stopping just beside Palmer's hand. It rocked back and forth for a moment, making a little sound that, in the now-silent bar, seemed almost deafening.

"Pick it up," Aubrey said to Palmer.

Palmer looked at the pistol. A vein was jumping in his neck, and those who were close enough to him could see his hands shaking.

"Do it," Aubrey said again.

"No, I ain't goin' to. No matter what you do, you can't make me fight."

"I'm counting to three," Aubrey said. "When I get to three, you had better reach for that gun because I'm going to pull mine."

"No, I told you!"

"One," Aubrey said coldly.

"I said no!"

"Two."

Suddenly Palmer made a desperate claw for the pistol. Aubrey smiled, because this was exactly what he had wanted Palmer to do. It was obvious, now, that it was a fair fight. He had told the cowboy he would count to three and, here Palmer was, cheating, trying to draw the gun before three.

Because the pistol was lying on the bar and not in a holster at his side, Palmer was at a distinct disadvantage. The gun would be much more difficult to pick up, than it would have been to draw.

"Three," Aubrey said, finishing the count, even as Palmer was making a desperate grab for the pistol.

Aubrey pulled his own gun then. He held it for a second, then looked around at all the others in the bar as if emphasizing that he was being more than fair. Then, just as Palmer brought the gun around, Aubrey fired. His bullet caught Palmer in the neck and Palmer dropped his gun, unfired, and clutched his throat. He fell back against the bar, then slid down, dead before he reached the floor.

Aubrey looked around the saloon, a broad smile on his face. "Well, so much for the loud-mouthed Mr. Palmer," he said. "Anyone else have anything to say?"

Everyone studied their glass or bottle, avoiding Aubrey's eyes.

"Aubrey Stiles kilt 'im fair and square, and you all

seen it," Townsen shouted. "Anyone plannin' on sayin' it was anything other than a fair fight?"

"I seen it too," Bean added. "The cowboy went for the gun first. Fact is, he cheated. He started reachin' for it before Aubrey counted to three."

The sound of the gunshot brought two or three outsiders into the saloon, including Marshal Jackson. Jackson saw Palmer sitting down against the bar, his eyes open and sightless, his hand clenched tightly around the unfired pistol. Then he saw Aubrey standing in the middle of the saloon floor, looking smug and defiant.

"Oh, hell," Jackson said quietly. "I might have known you would have something to do with this."

"Look in Palmer's hand, Marshal," Townsen said. "If Aubrey hadn't shot him, he would've shot Aubrey."

"Is that the way it was?" Jackson asked the others. When no one answered, Jackson asked the bartender directly. "Gus, is he calling it right?"

"You heard what Townsen and Bean said," Gus replied.

"You know them two. Aubrey could say the sun set in the east, and Townsen and Bean would swear to it. Now I'm asking you. How did it happen?"

"Palmer ain't got nobody to blame but his ownself," Gus said. "He come in here lookin' for trouble."

"Then you're backin' up Aubrey? You are saying he killed Palmer in self-defense?"

Gus looked at the others in the bar but, as before, none of them would return his gaze. No one seemed willing to comment.

"I guess you could call it self-defense," Gus said. "Palmer was tryin' to throw down on him, but it would'a taken him till next Sunday to do it."

"But, it was self-defense?" Jackson asked.

Gus sighed. "Yeah, it was self-defense."

Jackson looked at Aubrey. "One of these days, Aubrey, you're goin' to run up against someone who ain't a pushover. When you do, I'll be takin' your body over to the undertaker's, then ridin' out to tell your pa."

"I wouldn't be worryin' 'bout anything like that happening," Aubrey said.

"Oh, it'll happen," Jackson said. "I don't know when, or where, but it'll happen." He looked toward a couple of Rocking H hands. "He belongs to you boys," he said. "Take him over to the undertaker. I'll come along to make the arrangements."

The two cowboys picked up their fallen friend and carried him out the door, followed by the marshal.

"Ha!" Aubrey said after the marshal left. "Jackson thinks there might be someone around who can put me on the floor. Anyone got any idea who that might be?" He whipped his gun out and spun it around on his finger. "Anybody in here want to try that little deed?" He waved the gun around the room and as it passed, the men either ducked or averted their eyes. Aubrey laughed again, then he put the gun away. "I didn't think so."

"You the fastest there is, Aubrey. They ain't nobody goin' to tangle with you," Townsen said.

"Yeah, nobody," Bean added. "You're too good."

Excitedly, Aubrey tossed down the rest of his whiskey, then he stood up. "I'm goin' down to Big Sal's Place," he said. "I need me a woman."

"What about us?" Townsen asked.

"What about you? You got money enough for a woman?"

Townsen and Bean looked at each other sheepishly. They had hoped, by their hinting, to be included in the trip to Big Sal's. But that would have taken an advance from Aubrey, and he made no such offer.

"No," Townsen finally said. "We ain't got no money."

"You want us to wait here for you? We'll wait here if you want us to," Bean said, when it became obvious that Aubrey wasn't going to give them any money.

"Yeah, Aubrey, you know us. We'll do whatever you ask us to do," Townsen added.

"You two go on back out to the ranch. I'll see you later."

"Yeah," Bean said. "Me and Townsen'll go on out to the ranch."

"We'll see you later," Townsen called to Aubrey as he left the saloon.

Aubrey rode down to the end of the street, then tied his horse in front of Big Sal's Place. Big Sal met him in the front room.

"What do want, Aubrey?" she asked.

"What do I want? What do you mean, what do I want? What does anyone want when they come to a whore house?" Aubrey replied.

"I've already heard about what happened down at the saloon a while ago. I don't want any trouble like that in here."

Aubrey smiled. "You heard already, huh? Boy, news really travels fast." Looking around the salon, he saw Annie Bowman over by the piano, trying to make herself inconspicuous. "Annie," he said, pointing. "I want Annie. Tell her to come here."

Big Sal shook her head. "I don't tell any of my girls who they have to go with," she said. "It's up to them."

"Yeah?" Aubrey said. "Well, Annie's going to want to come with me, ain't you, girly?"

Hiding her fear behind a practiced smile, Annie nodded in the affirmative, then led Aubrey toward the stairs.

Chapter Eleven

It had been fifteen minutes since Aubrey Stiles took Annie upstairs with him, and Big Sal glanced up nervously. None of her girls had ever made any specific complaints about being with Aubrey, but she had noticed that none of them ever seemed anxious to be with him.

That in itself was a cause for curiosity, if not worry. Aubrey was the son of a very wealthy man, and Big Sal knew that it was the fantasy of many girls who were on the line to meet a wealthy man who could take them away from "the life." Aubrey seemed like an ideal candidate for such a fantasy, and yet every time he came around the girls tried to avoid him.

"What does a fella have to do to get a beer around this place?"

Looking up, Big Sal saw Gid Crockett. She smiled broadly at the bigger of the two brothers who had become very popular with the girls since taking rooms here.

"All you have to do is ask," Big Sal said.

"I'm asking," Gid said. "I've got that much dust in my craw that General Pemberton could have used it to build enough redoubts to hold out the entire Yankee Army."

Laughing, Big Sal drew a mug of beer and handed it to him.

"Is Annie around?" Gid asked.

"Busy," Big Sal answered, without elaboration. "Sorry."

"That's all right, she has to make a living just like everyone else."

"You boys haven't been staying in your rooms much, lately," Big Sal said. "You aren't giving them up, are you?"

"No," Gid answered. "We've been keeping busy, but it's nice knowing they're here when we can get around to them."

"Were you down at the saloon for all the excitement earlier?" Big Sal asked.

"What excitement?" Gid asked as he took another swallow of his beer.

"A cowboy named Palmer got himself shot."

Gid wiped the foam from his lips with the back of his hand. "Murder? Or fair fight?"

"They're calling it a fair fight, but from what I hear, there wasn't much fair about it. Aubrey Stiles goaded the cowboy into it."

"I've known a lot of men like Aubrey Stiles," Gid said. "They usually end up goading the wrong person into a fight, but not until they've killed their share of poor dumb bastards who didn't have enough sense to stay away from them."

Annie came down the stairs and went over to the bar, where she picked up a bottle and two glasses. Seeing her, Gid smiled and started toward her. "Hi, Annie," he said.

"I'm ... I'm busy, Gid," Annie replied, turning away from him as he approached her. "I just came down to get a bottle and a couple of glasses."

"That's all right. I'm in no hurry. I'll just have a couple of beers and wait. Come on back down when ..." Gid paused in mid-sentence, noticing then, that one of Annie's eyes was red and swollen.

"My god! What happened to you?" he asked.

"Nothing," Annie said, putting her hand up to cover the eye and making an even more pronounced effort to turn away from him.

"Don't tell me nothing. You've got as big a shiner there as I've ever seen on anyone."

"I have to go. He'll be waiting on his whiskey," Annie said, starting toward the stairs.

"Who'll be waiting?" Gid asked.

"Just.. .just one of the customers, that's all."

By now, Big Sal had come over to join in the conversation. When she saw Annie's red and puffed eye, she sucked in her breath through her teeth. "Oh, honey, what happened to you?" Big Sal asked. "Did Aubrey hit you?" Big Sal reached up to touch Annie's eye, but Annie pulled away from her.

"No, please, Big Sal," Annie said. "I don't want any trouble."

"What's going on, Annie?" Gid asked. He looked upstairs.

"Nothing, really," Annie answered.

"I'm going up there to tell him his time is up." Big Sal started toward the stairs.

"No, don't!" Annie said. "It's all right, nothing is going on." She reached out to grab Big Sal. "Nothing, honest. Please, leave it alone. You saw what he did to that cowboy. I wouldn't want him doing anything like that to you."

"Honey, what kind of house would I be running if I didn't look out for my girls? You don't have to go back up there. Not if he's hurting you."

"It'll be all right," Annie insisted. "I just don't want any more trouble, that's all."

Annie started for the stairs, but by the time she reached the bottom step, Aubrey, wearing only his trousers and a gun belt, appeared at the railing on the upper balcony.

"Hey, you! Bitch!" he shouted down at the girl. "I sent you down there to get a bottle of whiskey, not to have a quilting bee. You've been down there long enough. Get back up here!"

"Aubrey, she's already been up there long enough," Big Sal called up to him.

"What do you mean, she's been up here long enough?"

"Well, you know how it is," Big Sal answered, forcing a laugh. "I mean, Annie is a working girl. There are other gents in here wantin' her time, too. I can't let one man just have all her time. Why, how'd it be if you were waitin' on her right now?"

"Yeah? Is there anyone down here that's waitin' on her?"

There were nearly half a dozen customers standing around in the open salon, or sitting on one of the sofas with the other girls, but none of them spoke up.

"See what I mean?" Aubrey asked with an expansive wave of his hand. "They don't nobody but me want her, 'cause she's nothin' but a worthless slut. Now, you get back up here."

Annie shut her eyes tightly, squeezing out a tear. Gid watched her as she started toward the stairs. She took no more than a couple of steps, then she stopped. "No," she said. "No, I'm not coming back upstairs."

"The hell you ain't. I paid for you! You belong to me."

Annie clenched her fists and shook her head. "No, I don't belong to you. Your time is up."

"My time is up when I say my time is up."

Annie put her hand down in a dress pocket, then pulled out two pieces of silver.

"Here is your money," she said. "I'll give it back to you."

Aubrey pulled his pistol and pointed it toward Annie.

"I don't want my money, bitch. I want you. Now you get back up here or else I'm goin' to put a bullet right between your eyes."

"Annie, if you're not busy now, I'd like a little of your time," Gid said. He spoke the words as calmly as if he had just come into the house, as if none of this drama was being played. He had not said anything before now, because he figured that if Annie was dumb enough to voluntarily go back upstairs, then he wasn't going to try and stop her. But if she didn't want to go up, he was feeling just contrary enough to see to it that she didn' have to.

Aubrey looked toward Gid. When he recognized him, his face twisted into a grotesque smile.

"Well, if it isn't Mr. Crockett. I thought the Cattlemen's Association hired you and your brother to hunt down rustlers. Why aren't you out doing your job?"

"My brother is on the job. I decided to come in for a drink," Gid

said. "And maybe spend a little time with a woman."

"Yeah? Well, not with this woman. She's comin' back up to me."

"I don't think she wants to do that, and as a matter of fact, I don't want her to do it either."

"What the hell do I care what she wants?" Aubrey sneered. "She's got no choice. Neither do you, Mister Gid Crockett. It is Gid, isn't it? I know all about you Crockett brothers. Will is the oldest, and he is the fastest with a gun. You are the biggest, and the fastest with your fists. But your fists aren't going to do you any good, right now, Gid Crockett. You may have noticed that I happen to be holding a gun in my hand."

"Oh, yeah, I see the gun," Gid said. "But what are you going to do with it?"

"What do you mean what am I going to do with it?" Aubrey answered, obviously exasperated by Gid's question.

"The gun is pointing at the girl," Gid said. "But she's not your problem ... I am. If you move it toward me, I'm going to kill you. If you shoot her, I'm going to kill you. If you so much as twitch, I'm going to kill you. The only way you are going to get out of this alive is to drop your gun, right now."

"What?" Aubrey asked in disbelief. "Are you crazy?"

"Oh, you're right, by the way, about my brother being faster with a gun than I am. Now me? Well, I'm not all that fast."

Aubrey's cocky smile broadened.

"But I am fast enough to kill you," Gid added. "So,

what will it be? Are you going to drop the gun, or are you going to die?"

With a shout of rage, Aubrey swung his gun toward Gid and fired. The bullet slammed into the piano just alongside him, causing the strings to hum. At the same time, in one motion, Gid had his own gun out and he fired back just as Aubrey loosed a second shot.

Aubrey's second shot smashed into the overhead chandelier, scattering shards of glass, but doing no further damage. He didn't get off a third shot because Gid made his only shot count.

Aubrey dropped his gun over the rail and it fell with a clatter to the floor, twelve feet below. He grabbed his chest, then turned his hand out and looked down in surprise and disbelief as his palm began filling with his own blood. His eyes rolled back in his head and he pitched forward, crashing through the railing then turning over once in mid-air before he landed heavily on his back alongside his dropped gun.

Aubrey lay motionless on the floor with open, but sightless eyes staring toward the ceiling. Big Sal's patrons had scattered when the first shot was fired, but now they began edging back toward the body. Up on the second floor landing, a half-dozen girls and their customers, in various stages of undress, moved quickly to the smashed railing to look down on the scene.

Gunsmoke from the three charges merged to form a large, acrid-bitter cloud to spread over the salon below, and project its pungent odor into all the rooms above.

"Now, there lies one son of a bitch that needed killing," one of Big Sal's patrons said, kicking gently at Aubrey's still form with the toe of his dust-covered boot.

The shots had been heard outside and several people ran into Big Sal's Place to see what had happened. One of those who arrived was Marshal Jackson.

Seeing that the dead man was Aubrey Stiles, he stopped and shook his head. "I told the son of a bitch this was going to happen," he said. "I just didn't figure it was going to happen so soon." Jackson looked over at Gid, who had already put his gun away and was leaning against the piano. "I won't even ask if you're the one who did it. I figure you're the only one who could have."

"It was a fair fight, Marshal," Big Sal said. And, whereas before those in the saloon had been silent when Jackson attempted to solicit information about the killing of Palmer, everyone who had witnessed this fight was more than willing to testify.

"Damndest thing I ever saw, Marshal. Aubrey already had his gun out," one of the witnesses said.

"You need someone to give a statement, I'll be willin' to," another added

"Me too," Big Sal said.

"I don't reckon I'll be needing any statements," the marshal said, smiling at Gid. "I'm not even goin' to ask any questions about this one."

By now all the patrons had gathered around Aubrey's body and a few of the more curious were even squatting beside it to get a closer look.

"Where you reckon his hat and shirt is?" one of the men asked.

"More'n likely still up in the girl's room," another answered.

"I reckon Doc Stiles will be wantin' his son's stuff," Big Sal said.

Jackson nodded, then sighed. "I sure ain't lookin' forward to tellin' Doc Stiles that his son got himself killed." He pointed to two of the bystanders. "You two men get him over to the undertaker so he can get started on a coffin for him. That is, soon as he finishes the one he's workin' on now."

"We'll take him over there, Marshal, but if this keeps up, I'm thinkin' the undertaker is goin' to have to start puttin' people on."

The two men Jackson assigned to the job picked up Aubrey's body, one under the shoulders, the other at the feet. Aubrey sagged badly in the middle and they had to struggle to carry him. A couple of the other patrons held the door open while the two men carried him out across the porch, and down into the street.

"Ladies, and your gentlemen friends," Big Sal said after the body was outside. "I think we all need a drink."

The girls and their customers hurried over to the side bar where Big Sal began pouring. Jackson stepped over to Gid and nodded at the happy throng.

"Hell of a note, isn't it, when a man's death is cause for a celebration?"

"I've got a feeling that someone like Aubrey would rather go out this way than not be noticed at all," Gid said.

"You're probably right," Jackson replied.

"Gid, I want to thank you for what you did," Annie said, coming up to him then.

"It needed doin'," Gid replied.

"You're always welcome in my bed, Gid Crockett," Annie said. "But... if you don't mind ... I think I'm going to ask Big Sal to let me be alone tonight."

"I don't mind," Gid said.

"Well, I guess I'd best be going out to Doc Stiles's ranch to tell him what happened," Jackson said, setting his empty beer mug on the bar.

"You want me to go with you?" Gid asked.

"What?" Jackson replied, surprised that Gid would even make the offer. "Are you serious?"

"Yes, I'm serious."

Jackson shook his head. "No, I don't think that would

be a good idea."

"Whatever you say," Gid said, returning to his beer as Jackson left, chuckling in amusement over the offer.

With Aubrey's body gone and the excitement over, most of the girls and their customers soon returned to the sofas and chairs to resume their drinking and conversation. Whatever subject had held their attention before the shooting, the shooting itself was the theme of all the conversations now. It was played and replayed a dozen times over. Once or twice, a couple of the women approached Gid, signaling that even though Annie was withholding her services for the night, they were available.

Gid had actually come in tonight for a quiet drink and some time with a woman, but the events of the last several minutes had cooled his ardor. Now, all he wanted to do was have a few drinks and be left alone.

Big Sal, sensing that, made certain that Gid got his wish.

Chapter Twelve

The next evening the Cattlemen's Association met in an emergency session. Doc Stiles had the floor. The expression on his face was pinched, and drawn with sorrow over the death of his son.

"I know that Aubrey could sometimes be difficult. But he was my son. And now he's dead, shot down by one of the very men we hired to protect us."

"Stiles, I'm sorry that he was your son. And I'm sorry that you are grieved by this," Holeman said. "But not half an hour before he was killed, Aubrey shot down one of my best men ... practically in cold blood."

"Everyone who saw it says it was a fair fight," Stiles said.

"Everyone said what they thought your son wanted them to say because they were afraid of him. Now that he's dead the true story has come out. Aubrey forced the fight."

"Maybe so, but it was a fight between young, hot-blooded men, and it had nothing at all to do with the problem of rustling. Don't you see what I'm getting at?"

"No, I don't think I do."

"What I mean is, this fight may very well have happened whether Crockett was here or not. It was part of the natural order of things. But Gid Crockett's killing Aubrey wasn't." Stiles ran his hand through his gray, curly hair. "I don't know, I feel responsible, somehow. I mean, here I am, one of those who brought the Crocketts in here and what have they done except create an atmosphere of killing? Why, do you realize that since Will and Gid Crockett arrived there have been ten killings? Ten men dead in just a few days, and one of them is my son."

"And one of the ten, your son killed," one of the other ranchers pointed out.

"I know, I know," Stiles said. He pinched his nose and was quiet for a moment, as if trying to compose himself. Finally, he sighed. "The point is, whether anyone is sorry to see my son gone or not, you have to admit that ten dead in a few days is unconscionable. And I can't help but believe it is the Crocketts' general disregard for life that has created this atmosphere. What manner of beasts have we unleashed on our people?"

"What did you expect, Stiles?" Chamberlain asked. "Did you expect the rustlers to leave just because we hired someone to root 'em out?"

"I don't know," Stiles replied. He put his hand to his forehead and sat down in his chair. "I don't know what I expected. But I didn't plan on starting a bloodbath. And I didn't plan on losing my son. I truly regret having been a party to the hiring of the Crockett brothers.

"And as for my son? Perhaps I should have done something about him. I just continued to nurture the hope that one day he would stop pretending to be a gunfighter and turn into a productive citizen."

"For god's sake, Stiles, your son had already killed two people before he shot Palmer. He wasn't pretending to be a gunfighter. He was one."

"Yes, as much as I hate to admit it, I suppose he was. That's why I didn't have a funeral for him. I know how all of you felt about him, and I didn't want to put you out by asking you to come. Still, he was my son, and I loved him. I buried him this morning, out at the ranch, alongside his ma."

"What about you, Holeman? Where are you plannin' on buryin' Palmer?" one of the others asked.

"In Boot Hill tomorrow, just after noon," Holeman answered. "We don't have a cemetery out at the Rocking H, but I'll be lettin' all the boys off to come into town for the funeral. I've already paid for the coffin and took care of the preacher. He's all set to read over the body."

"Me an' my boys'll be there," Ashby said.

"So will we," Woods added.

"Yes, I imagine most of us will be. But, gentlemen, if you don't mind, I'd like to suggest that we get back to the topic of our discussion," Stiles said. "As you know, I am concerned about the bloodshed we've unleashed in our valley and I have a question for this group. Which do we value more? Is it property, or human life?"

"What are you gettin' at?"

"I think it's about time we faced up to our responsibilities. A killing fever has been spread over the land and the Crocketts are the ones who brought the fever to us."

"You know, gents, Doc may have a point," Ashby said. "When you think about it, we were a pretty peaceful town until the Crocketts come along. Ever since they arrived there's been a lot of killing."

"Okay, but let's look at it," Chamberlain said. "Surely you aren't saying that the men who burned my ranch didn't deserve killing? Or the three who were killed when they came back the second time? Because, those are the only deaths the Crocketts are responsible for and as far as I'm concerned, it's good riddance to all of them. And one more thing. Not one cow has been stolen since the Crocketts arrived."

"Chamberlain is right about that, gents. The rustlin' has stopped," Woods said. "You've got to consider that."

"They're afraid to come out at night because they know one of the Crocketts might be out there, just like a night hawk, waiting to pounce on them from the dark."

"I know how you men feel," Stiles said. "Hell, if you remember, I was as much for hirin' them as any of you. But now, I'm beginning to wonder if we did the right thing."

"So, where does that leave us?" Ashby asked.

"That leaves us with a decision to make," Stiles said.

"Hell, if you're trying to figure out whether or not we should keep them, then I say, let's bring it to a vote. But if we're going to vote, I'm telling you here and now, I'm going to vote yes," Chamberlain said.

"I am too," Holeman said. "I have to admit that the killing does bother me and I think we should keep an eye on it. But, so far, they haven't killed anyone who didn't need killing." He looked over at Stiles. "I'm sorry, Doc, but from all accounts, that includes your son."

Stiles nodded, but said nothing.

"So, for now, I'd say let's keep them around," Holeman concluded.

"I vote for them to stay," Ashby added.

"Me too," Woods said.

"Doc?" Chamberlain asked. "You're the only one we haven't heard from."

Stiles sighed. "All right, I suppose I'll vote to keep them too," he agreed. "I just hope we aren't making a big mistake."

Chamberlain smiled. "Then it is unanimous. The Crocketts stay on the job."

Will and Gid were unaware that the Cattlemen's Association was conducting a meeting to decide their fate. Even if they had been aware, they would have been unconcerned. They were men with a singleness of purpose and their purpose was to break up the rustling ring and bring in Doran. They were going to do that now, regardless of whether or not they had the endorsement of the Association.

Though they kept their rooms at Big Sal's Place, they found that they were actually spending most of their nights out on the prairie. That was because the people they were chasing did most of their work at night, and if they wanted to catch them, they had to be out there with them.

Gid killed a rabbit and spitted it over an open flame to cook for their supper. It was during supper that Will realized they were being watched.

"Gid," he said. "We've got company."

Gid nodded, but said nothing. Then, showing no sign that they knew that anyone was out there, they extinguished the fire, then spread out their bedrolls as if they were about to go to bed. They carefully placed their boots at the foot of the bedroll, and their hats at the top. After that they crawled down into the blankets and lay there for a moment, in the darkness.

"You ready, Gid?" Will whispered.

"I'm ready," Gid whispered back.

Quietly, the two brothers snaked their way out of their bedrolls, then slid down into a small gully that ran adjacent to their camp. Pulling their pistols, they teased the hammers back, then inched up to the top of the gully to stare through the darkness toward the bedrolls.

From there, with their boots and hats in position, it looked exactly as if they were still in the blankets, sound asleep. Will smiled in grim approval. If the campsite looked that way to him, it would look that way to whoever was dogging them.

They waited.

Out on the prairie a coyote howled.

An owl hooted.

A falling star flashed across the dark sky.

A soft, evening breeze moaned through the mesquite.

And still they waited.

Almost a full hour after Will and Gid had "gone to bed," the night was lit up by the great flame-patterns produced by the discharge of a couple of shotguns. The double roar of the shotguns boomed loudly, and Will saw dust and bits of cloth fly up from the bedrolls where charges of buckshot tore into them. Had he and Gid been there, the impact debris would have been bone and flesh rather than dust and cloth, and they would be dead men.

"Now!" Will shouted.

At Will's shout, he and Gid shot in the direction of the muzzle flashes.

"Oh, you sons of bitches! You're a couple of smart ones, you are," a voice shouted, almost jovially. The voice was not near the muzzle flash and Will knew that their would-be assailants must have fired and moved. Whoever they were, they weren't amateurs.

Even as Will thought this, he realized that the assailants could use the flame pattern from their own pistols as targets.

"Gid, move!" he shouted, as he threw himself to the right, just as the shotguns roared a second time. Though none of the pellets hit them, they dug into the earth where the two brothers had been but an instant earlier and sent a spray of stinging sand into his face. Will fired again, again aiming at the muzzle-blast, though by now he knew there would be no one there. A moment later he heard the sound of retreating hoof beats and he knew that their attackers were riding away.

"You hit, Gid?"

"No. You?"

"No."

"Who do you think it was?"

"My guess is, it has to be a couple of Doran's men," Will answered.

As Townsen and Bean approached the entrance to Hidden Canyon, Townsen removed his hat, then waved it broadly across the top of his head. He put it on, then took it off and repeated the gesture. A moment later they saw a flashing mirror, indicating that they could proceed. When they reached the innermost part of the valley, they saw a bull-like man with a bald head and a heavy, hairless brow, waiting for him.

"Hello, Doran," Townsen said. "Surprised to see us?"

"No," Doran answered. "I heard about Stiles getting' his fool self shot down."

"After all the time we wasted with that son of a bitch, for him to go and do a dumb thing like that," Townsen said.

One of the women of the outlaws' camp squealed happily, and came running toward Townsen.

"It wasn't a waste of time. You boys done a good job of keepin' us up on what was goin' on," Doran said. "What about the Crocketts?"

Bean shook his head. "They're a couple of smart critters, all right. We trailed 'em last night, and I thought we had 'em, but they tricked us."

Had any of the range cowboys, or anyone from town,

been present now, they would have been shocked by what they were seeing. Gone were the groveling personalities Guy Townsen and Russ Bean had adopted.

"So, what do you want us to do now?" Townsen asked. "Stay or go back outside?"

"I don't know, I haven't decided yet. Let me think on it a while."

"You had breakfast, Guy?" the woman who was hanging on Townsen asked.

"No."

"Come with me. I'll take care of you."

The woman made no offer to feed Bean, and as Townsen walked away with her, he showed no concern for the fact that his friend hadn't eaten either.

Such behavior didn't bother Bean though. Had the situation been reversed, he would have done the same thing. Without giving it a second thought, he walked over toward the fire where a large, blue-steel coffeepot hung by a wire. Picking up a chipped and stained cup, he bumped the dust out of it, then tipped the pot over to pour a stream of thick, black liquid. As he raised the cup to his lips and blew on the steaming coffee, he looked around.

"Where's Bella?"

"Bella?"

"Yeah, you know the one. Big black eyes? She was Jake Simmons's woman."

"Oh, yeah, I know the one you mean," Doran said. "She's over there, by that kettle. Don't know why you're interested, though. She's still cryin' over Jake getting' hisself killed the other night."

"I know. But she's goin' to need someone to comfort her. It might as well be me." Even as Bean spoke, Bella caught his glance and smiled coquettishly back at him. "See what I mean?" he said, starting toward her.

It wasn't Bean's looks or personality that Bella was attracted to. With Jake dead, she had no sponsor. There was no charity in the outlaw camp. Everyone had to pull their own weight, or else have a personal sponsor, or they couldn't stay. And, though no one had told her directly, Bella was smart enough to realize that it was unlikely anyone who knew as much about the outlaws as she knew, would be allowed to just leave.

An hour later, behind a rock outcropping, Bean was looking down at Bella as he pulled his pants back on. Bella hadn't taken her clothes off, but had merely pulled her dress up. Her dress was still bunched around her waist, as she made no effort to cover herself. Her head was turned to one side, and she was crying softly.

"What the hell you crying for?" Bean asked gruffly.

"For no reason," Bella answered. "Sometimes, a woman cries for no reason." She couldn't tell him that his rough, unskilled lovemaking just underscored how much she would miss Jake Simmons.

"Russ?" Townsen called, coming toward them. When Townsen saw Bella lying on the ground behind the rock, he chuckled. "You finished?"

"Yeah," Bean answered. "What is it?"

"Doran has a job for us."

There were several men gathered around Doran when Townsen and Bean walked up to join them.

"You get your business finished?" Doran asked Bean. The others sniggered knowingly.

"Yeah," Bean answered gruffly.

"Good," Doran said. Then, addressing all of them, Doran continued. "Boys, we're goin' to pay a visit to the Rocking H. I figure we'll drop in along about noon ... when everyone on the ranch is in town at the cemetery, buryin' that cowboy that Stiles shot. There won't be a livin' soul left out at the ranch. We can just ride in and help ourselves to as many cows as we want to drive away."

Vic Armstrong chuckled. "Yeah," he said. "Yeah, that's a good idea. I got to hand it to you, Doran. Takin' them cows is goin' to be as easy as takin' candy from a baby."

Chapter Thirteen

The sun was high overhead at the Rocking H ranch, a brilliant white orb fixed in the bright blue sky in such a position as to take away all the spots of shade where the cattle would normally congregate. With the shade denied them, the cows had all moved down to mill about in and along the banks of Drinkwater Creek.

Drinkwater Creek was what made the Rocking H a ranch instead of a stretch of barren desert. Some of the cows had come to water, while others were there just to be nearer the band of green grass that followed the stream on its zig-zagging path across the otherwise brown floor of the valley.

The main building and the outhouses of the ranch sat empty under the blows of the midday sun. Everyone on the ranch, Holeman's family and all his hands, had gone into town for Palmer's funeral. Palmer had been a man who never made more work for others by shirking his own responsibilities. As a result he was well liked by everyone who knew him. Almost as if it were out of respect for him, the ranch was quiet, with even the dogs and chickens maintaining their silence.

Doran was right when he said that every hand on the place would be in town for Palmer's funeral. He was wrong, however, when he said that there wouldn't be a soul on the place. Anticipating exactly what Doran had in mind, Will and Gid were waiting for them. The only question was, from which way would they come? To cover that, Will sent Gid to the north side of the ranch, while he waited on the south. The size of the ranch was such that they were about three miles apart, too far to signal each other by any means other than gunshot, which they didn't want to do because that would give away their positions.

Will was standing on a rock, sucking on the sweet root of a stem of grass, when he saw four men come riding in, moving across the valley floor as leisurely as if they had all day to accomplish their job.

As Will watched their approach, he thought of how easy it would be to set up an ambush. From this angle and range he could cut down a couple of them before they had any idea what was going on. Then he could take out the remaining two before they had time to get away. But he knew he wasn't going to do that though. It would stick in his craw.

Will jumped down from the rock, then rode toward the stream where nearly a hundred cows were watering. He chose a route of approach that protected him from observation by a long finger of ridge line that ran parallel to Drinkwater Creek.

"How many are we goin' to cut out?" he heard one of the rustlers ask.

"Well, they's four of us. We should be able to drive 'em all... at least the ones that's right here," another answered.

"You know, this beats it though. I mean, I went into this business in the first place 'cause I didn't want to punch cows, and what am I doin'? I'm punchin' cows."

The others laughed, then one of them answered, "Yeah, but our cut is a dollar a head for ever'one of these cows we move. You know any cowboys who are makin' that kind of money?"

"No, I reckon not."

They were close enough now that Will could hear them quite clearly. That meant they were close enough to confront. He crested the ridge. There, no more than twenty yards in front of him, he saw the four riders getting ready to move in on Holeman's cows. He pulled his pistol.

"Why don't you fellas just hold it right there?" he called.

"What the hell? Where'd you come from?" Townsen hissed, startled by Will's sudden appearance.

"Well, Townsen and Bean," Will said. "I see you didn't take long to find somebody new to suck up to."

The two erstwhile Stiles riders glared at him, but said nothing.

"Shuck your guns and raise your hands," Will said. "We're goin' into town."

"For what?" Bean asked. "We ain't doin' nothin' but takin' a ride."

Suddenly there was an angry buzz, then the "thocking" sound of a heavy bullet tearing into flesh. A fountain of blood squirted up from the neck of Will's horse and the animal went down on its front knees, then collapsed onto its right side. It was almost a full second after the strike of the bullet before the heavy boom of a distant rifle reached Will's ears.

The fall pinned Will's leg under his horse. He also dropped his pistol on the way down, and now it lay just out of reach of his grasping fingers.

"What the hell? Who's that shooting?" Bean shouted, pulling hard on the reins of his horse who, though not hit, was spooked by the sight of seeing Will's horse go down. "Is it one of our men? Who is it?"

"Who the hell cares?" Townsen shouted back. "Look at him! Crockett is pinned down. Here's my chance to kill the son of a bitch!" He raised his gun and fired at Will.

Though Will's right leg was still pinned, he was able

to flip his left leg over the saddle and lay down behind his horse, thus providing him with some cover. Townsen's bullet dug into his saddle and sent up a little puff of dust, but did no further damage.

"Shit!" Townsen said. "I can't get to him from this angle."

"Come on!" Bean called. "Let's get the hell out of here while the getting is good!"

"Not until I put a bullet in Crockett!" Townsen insisted. He slapped his legs against the side of his horse and moved around to get a better shot at Will.

Will made one more desperate grab for his pistol but it was still out of reach. His rifle, however, was in the saddle sheath on the side of the horse which was on the ground and Will could see about six inches of the stock sticking out. He grabbed it and was gratified when it pulled free. He jerked it from the sheath and jacked a shell into the chamber, just as Townsen came around to get into position to shoot him.

"Goodbye, Mr. Crockett," Townsen said, raising his pistol and taking careful aim. The smile left his face as he saw the business end of Will's rifle raise up, then spit a finger of flame. The .44-40 bullet from Will's rifle hit Townsen just under the chin, then exited the back of his head along with a pink spray of blood and bone as Townsen tumbled off his horse.

"He got Townsen!" one of the men said.

"That's his own damn fault. Let's get the hell out of here!" Bean shouted.

Bean and the two men with him were riding away hard now, not even bothering to look back to see what happened to Townsen. In the meantime, another bullet whistled by from the distant rifle. When Will located the source of the shooting, he saw a mounted man with one leg thrown casually across his saddle. Using that leg to provide a stable firing platform, the shooter raised his rifle to fire again. There was a flash of light, the man rolled back from the recoil, then the bullet whizzed by so close to Will's head that it made his ears pop. All this before the report of the rifle actually reached him. With a gasp of disbelief, Will realized that this man was firing from at least one thousand yards away! Will fired back, not with any expectation of actually hitting his target, but merely to show his enemy that he wasn't completely helpless.

In a way, Will was running a bluff, because he was practically helpless. He was still trapped under his horse and he knew if he didn't get himself free soon, whoever was shooting at him would be able to change locations and catch Will in an exposed position. Will tried again to pull his leg free but he was unable to do so. Then he got an idea. He stuck the stock of the rifle just under the horse's side and grabbed the barrel.

Using the rifle as a lever, he pushed up and wedged just enough space between the horse's flesh and the ground to allow him to slip his leg free.

His first fear was that his leg might be broken, but as soon as he pulled it out, he knew that it wasn't. The blood circulation was cut off however, and when he tried to stand he promptly fell back down again. As it was, that turned out to be a blessing, for another bullet whistled by at that very moment, at the precise place where his head would have been, had he been standing.

Crawling on his belly, Will slithered and twisted his way down to the stream. He reached the bank, then got down into the water just as another bullet ploughed into the dirt beside him. Will twisted around behind the bank and looked back up toward the place where the shots were coming from. With the stream bank providing him cover and a rifle in his hands, he was no longer a sitting duck. Whoever was after him realized this as well, for Will saw him put his rifle back in the saddle sheath, then turn and ride away as casually as if he were riding down main street. And why not? There was no way Will was going to hit him at this distance, at least not with a .44-40 Winchester.

Will heard the hooves of a fast approaching horse, and he turned quickly to confront the new challenge. He breathed a sigh of relief, however, when he saw that it was Gid.

"Will! Are you all right?" Gid called.

"Yeah," Will called back. He pointed to Townsen's horse which had trotted away during the shooting but was back now, peacefully cropping grass. "Grab that horse, Gid. I'll need a mount."

"What happened?'" Gid asked a moment later as he returned with Townsen's horse.

As Will switched his saddle with Townsen's, he told Gid about the long distance shooter.

"Was he one of Doran's men?" Gid asked.

"I don't think so," Will replied. "They ran from him."

"Well, that's strange. Who the hell would be shooting at both of you?"

"Whoever he is, he's one hell of a shot," Will said.

Once they were mounted, they rode up to the top of the distant ridge to the spot where the shooting had come from. Will wanted to have a look at the place where the gunman had been.

A flash of sunlight led him to the first sign. When he picked it up he saw that it was the brass casing of a .45-caliber shell of a type made especially for the Whitworth. The Whitworth, Will knew, was a hexagonal-shaped, long-barrel rifle which, when fitted with a telescope, could be fired accurately at ranges up to 1,000 yards. It had been the preferred weapon of the long-distance sharpshooters during the War Between the States.

"You know anybody who owns such a gun?" Gid asked.

Will shook his head. "No, I don't. But if I ever see one sticking out of a saddle sheath, I plan to ask a few questions."

Laying aside the puzzle of who the long-distance shooter had been, the two brothers rode back down to where Townsen's body lay sprawled in death. Gid picked the rustler up and threw him across the saddle pommel in front of Will. Then they rode into town with him.

Boot Hill was located at the western end of town. Wagons and buggies were leaving the cemetery as the friends of Earl Palmer began returning to their own lives. The funeral service for Palmer was just breaking up as the Crocketts rode into town.

"That's eleven," someone said quietly as he saw Will and Gid ride by with Townsen's body draped across Will's horse. "Eleven men have been killed since them two Crocketts arrived in town."

Marshal Jackson stood on the little wooden sidewalk just in front of his office as Will flipped Townsen's body off. Townsen landed on his back in the dirt of the street, sending up a little cloud of dust. Several people were nearby and a few of them came over to stare at Townsen's body. His eyes were open and glazed, there was a small, black hole just under his chin, and a much larger one, with blood-matted hair, at the back of his head.

"It's Townsen," word went on down the street. Within moments, others were coming toward the marshal's office, anxious to get a look at the latest victim of the rapidly escalating death toll.

"You sort of wasted your time with that one, didn't you, Crockett?" the marshal said. "Townsen's no rustler. He rides for Doc Stiles."

"Not since yesterday, he didn't. He was ridin' for Doc Stiles, but after Aubrey got hisself killed, Townsen and Bean both quit," someone in the crowd said.

"Yeah, they didn't have Aubrey's ass to kiss anymore," one of the others said, and there was a nervous tittering of laughter.

Doc Stiles pushed his way through the crowd and looked down at Townsen's body, then up at Will and Gid.

"What'd you shoot him for? He was as harmless as they come. Why, without my son to tag along after, I doubt this boy could even go to the bathroom by himself."

"This 'boy,' as you call him, tried to kill me," Will said. "I killed him in self-defense. I had no choice."

"Why, he and Bean were afraid of their own shadows. It is hard for me to picture him throwing down on anyone. Especially going up against someone like you," Stiles said in a voice that indicated he didn't believe Will. "What do you suppose would make him do such a thing?"

"Let's just say that he found himself in what he thought was an advantageous position," Will explained. "Turns out he was wrong."

"I see. Uh, Mr. Crockett, perhaps it's about time we had a little talk. Just you, your brother, me, and the Cattlemen's Association." Looking around, Stiles saw Holeman, Chamberlain, Woods and Ashby in the crowd, and nodding at them, he invited them in to be a party to the conversation.

The Cattlemen's Association had its office next door to the marshal's office. The office had been closed during Palmer's funeral and the men had to wait for a moment while Doc Stiles unlocked the door. Once inside, they took their usual seats around the long conference table, with Doc Stiles in his position at the head, as the Association's president. As the office had been closed up for most of the day, it was quite hot and stuffy. One of the men raised a window to let in some air, and with the air came the odor of horse droppings from the street. To most of the townspeople the street odors were as unnoticeable as the other odors of the town ... the rotting garbage, the stale beer and whiskey from behind the saloons, the several dozen outhouses which reeked in the midday sun. To Will and Gid, who were used to the wide-open spaces, the smells of civilization were overpowering.

Doc Stiles took out a handkerchief and wiped his

face, then pointed to a couple of chairs, inviting the boys to be seated. Gid sat, but Will declined, leaning instead against the wall. He took out the makings and started rolling a cigarette.

"Is there a problem?" Will asked.

The others looked at Stiles, not only because he was the head of the Association, but because he was the one who had called the meeting.

Stiles drummed his fingers on the table for a moment, then answered Will's question.

"Yes, Mr. Crockett, there is a problem. We've already had one meeting to discuss the situation, and events are dictating that we have another. I have to tell you that we of the Association, as well as many of the citizens of the town, are becoming quite concerned with what seems to be an excessive amount of bloodshed. Every reward that the Association has paid so far has been paid for a body. Not once since you two arrived has a living prisoner been brought in for reward. That, despite the fact that the reward is just as high for those you bring in alive, as it is for those you bring in dead."

"We haven't killed anyone who wasn't trying to kill us," Will said. "And they have all been rustlers . . . the very people you are paying us to hunt down."

"What about my son?" Stiles asked. "He certainly wasn't a rustler. And neither was Townsen."

"I'm sorry about your son," Gid said. "But I didn't have any choice. He was trying to kill me."

"I know, I've heard from all the witnesses," Stiles said. "And much as it pains me to believe them, I do believe them. If I didn't believe them, you may rest assured, Mr. Crockett, that you would be dead by now."

"Your son may not have been a rustler, but I believe Townsen was," Will said. "I killed him on Holeman's ranch. And he was riding with three other men. There's no doubt in my mind but that they were out there to steal Holeman's cattle while everyone was at the funeral."

"Damn!" Holeman said, slamming his fist into his open hand.

"Crockett's right, Doc. It all makes sense. Of course the bastards would choose today to come."

"But Townsen?"

"He and Bean must've joined up with Doran," Holeman said. "Hell, you said it yourself, they both quit right after Aubrey was killed. And neither one of them had the gumption to do anything on their own. Hell they could be led around like a couple of puppy dogs."

"Just because a man lacks gumption, that shouldn't be enough cause to get him shot," Stiles said.

"I'm not sure that you knew Townsen and Bean as well as you thought you did," Will said.

"What do you mean?"

"The Townsen I saw out there on the range was not the poltroon you have been portraying. He was tough, vicious, and determined. He wanted to kill me, and he came at me, head on."

The ranchers laughed.

"To what do you attribute Townsen's sudden conversion from a coward to a warrior?"

"That's just it," Will said. "I don't think it was a sudden change."

"What do you mean?"

"I think he was always the man I saw. I think he was acting the part of a toady. I think he and Bean took all of you in. I think they were both working for Doran all along."

"You're just saying that, because you want to be paid for one more body," Doc Stiles suggested. "You've overstepped your bounds, Crockett. Both of you have. And I think we should discuss whether or not we are going to continue this arrangement."

"I don't," Chamberlain said.

"What do you mean?" Stiles asked, surprised by the comment.

"Doc, this is the second time you've called a meeting about this," Chamberlain said. "Now, we voted to keep them the last time and I'm willin' to bet we're going to vote to keep them this time. The truth is, I'm gettin' tired of holdin' a meeting every time someone gets themselves shot. I say they're doing a good job and I say let's leave them alone."

"I agree," Woods said, and Holeman concurred.

"Am I the only one worried about the excessive amount of killing going on around here?" Doc Stiles asked.

"As far as I'm concerned, it's not excessive as long as it's needed," Chamberlain said.

"But are we sure that it's needed?"

"We don't have any reason to believe that it isn't."

Doc Stiles sighed and leaned back in his chair. He pressed his hands together and studied Will and Gid for a long time before he spoke.

"Very well, we'll keep you on. However, for my own peace of mind, could I have your assurances that no more people will be killed?"

"I'm sorry, but we can't promise that," Will said.

"Then can I have your word that no more will be killed than is absolutely necessary?"

"I've already given my word on that," Will said. "I see no reason to do it again."

"He's right, Doc," Chamberlain said. "I told you, let's just leave them alone and let them go about their business."

"I agree with Chamberlain," Ashby said.

"Holeman? Woods?"

"I think they are doing a bang-up job," Holeman said.

"They've got my vote," Woods added.

"All right, all right, I'll go along with the majority." Stiles agreed. "But I want it clearly understood that I am on record as abhorring all the violence which I believe these men have spawned."

"We'll keep that in mind," Chamberlain said.

"Is that all?" Will asked.

"Yes."

"Good."

"All I have to say to you men is, keep up the good work," Holeman said. "If you hadn't been on the job, I would have lost a sizeable part of my herd."

"Yeah. I guess we owe you an apology and our thanks," Woods suggested.

Chapter Fourteen

"Beans again!" Armstrong growled as the fat Mexican woman spooned them onto his plate. "Is that all you ever have around here?"

"We have no more beef, senor," the cook said. "And the bacon, she is gone too."

"Well, now, this is a hell of a note, ain't it?" Armstrong complained as he walked over to sit at the rough-hewn table with half a dozen other men. "I mean we've rustled enough beef to start a full-sized stampede, but we ain't got so much as a mouthful of meat to lay alongside our beans."

"Quit your belly-achin'," Doran growled as he held his own plate out. "If you want meat for every meal, you can always go back to punchin' cows for thirty dollars a month and found. You're rustlin' cows because it pays more, not because it's an easy life."

"Perhaps you ain't noticed it lately, Doran, but we ain't

exactly been rustlin' a hell of a lot of cows, either. In fact, it's been quite a while since we've so much as took one steer and got away with it."

"Yeah," a man named Martin put in. "You said it'd be a piece of cake to go out to Chamberlain's place and take his herd. Well, we went out there. And we lost five men burnin' the place down and another three when we raided the ranch. They was good men too, ever' one of 'em. All that and for what? We didn't get so much as one cow."

"And we didn't get nothin' from the Rocking H, either, except Guy got hisself killed," Bean added.

"You got no room to talk, Bean," Doran growled. "You 'n Townsen lived the good life for a long time while we was in here livin' on beans and spit."

"What we need to do is get rid of the Crockett brothers," a man named Cleveland suggested.

"The problem is, the Crocketts ain't our only problem," Armstrong suggested. "Don't forget the son of a bitch who was shootin' at us from damn near a mile away."

"That was probably the other Crockett brother," Martin said. "There's two of 'em, remember, and we only had one of 'em trapped."

Armstrong shook his head. "No. Whoever it was that shot at us, was shootin' at Crockett too. Don't you remember? He's the one that killed Crockett's horse."

"Yeah, that's true, isn't it?" Martin said, stroking his

chin. "Well, I'm wondering now, just who that could be?"

"Well, whoever he was, he isn't our biggest problem. Our biggest problem is still the Crocketts. They have just about brought our rustlin' days to a halt," Armstrong said.

"It don't seem right that no more'n a couple of ordinary men could do that to us," Martin complained.

"Well, see, now there's the problem," Cleveland said. "Because them Crocketts ain't exactly what you would call ordinary men."

"What do you mean?" Martin asked.

"What I mean is, they're more like ghosts than regular men," Cleveland explained. "I mean, no matter where we go, they are there first... comin' in as silent as smoke, raisin' hell, then goin' away without so much as a scratch for all the shootin'."

"They've just been lucky so far, that's all."

"Lucky hell," Cleveland replied. "Luck ain't got nothin' to do with it. I'm here to tell you, they ain't no ordinary men."

"Problem with you, Cleveland, is they've got you spooked bad," Armstrong said. Armstrong looked over at Doran. "You've met them, Bean. What do you think about what Cleveland said?"

Bean spooned some beans onto his folded tortilla, then took a bite and chewed thoughtfully before he answered. "What do I think?" he repeated "I think Cleveland was right when he said we need to kill the sons of bitches. That's what I think."

"Easy enough to say ... not so easy to do," Cleveland said. "I don't figure either one of the Crocketts are the kind of man that dies easy."

"Bullshit. Put a bullet in their hide and they'll die just like ever'one else," Doran growled.

"Then how come we ain't been able to kill 'em?"

"We haven't tried," Doran said. "Except for Aubrey Stiles and Guy Townsen. And they don't count for much, because one of them was a blowhard and the other was a damn fool."

"Are you sayin' that you'd be willin' to go up against either one of 'em?" Martin asked Doran.

"Hell, no," Doran answered. "I ain't willin' to go up against them and I don't figure anybody else should have to, either."

"What do you mean? I thought you said they needed killin'."

"They do need killin'," Doran said. He smiled. "But what does goin' up against them have to do with it? What the hell, we don't need to make no sportin' contest out of this. We ain't like that fool Aubrey Stiles, tryin' to be known as the 'Fastest Gun in the West.' There don't none of us need to try it alone, and there ain't no need to face either one of them sons of bitches down. I mean, all that's needed is for someone to kill the bastards. If they're shot in the front or in the back, it don't make no difference. They'll be just as dead."

"Yeah," one of the others said. "Sneak up on the sons of bitches and shoot 'em in the back. That's the way to handle 'em."

"I got an idea how maybe to get this done," Doran said, wiping some of the dripping bean juice from his chin. "S'pose we all put one hundred dollars in a pot, just like as if we was playin' poker. If one man kills one of the Crocketts, half the money is his. If he kills both of 'em, all the money is his. And, if more than one winds up doin' it, then they'll split up the money."

"Yeah, that sounds like a good idea," Martin said. He stuck his hand into his pocket and pulled out a wad of bills. "Ante up, fellas. I don't need anybody to help me, the way I'm goin' to do it. And if I am the one that kills them both, then I want to see how much money I'm goin' to get."

Some distance away, a small man with blotchy red skin, watery blue eyes and a prominent hook nose was just approaching the town of Cochise Springs. The sun was down now, and the night creatures were calling to each other. A cloud passed over the moon, then moved away, bathing in silver the little town that rose up before him. Two dozen buildings, half of which spilled yellow light onto the ground out front, faced the town's single street. The biggest building at this edge of town was the livery stable, dark inside, though lighted from without by the town's only street lamp. The most brightly lit building was the town saloon.

The man, whose name was Wilson Hays, stopped his horse just at the edge of a little stand of cottonwood trees, then ground-hobbled him. He pulled his long-barreled Whitworth from the saddle sheath then unwrapped the special oiled cloth he kept around it. The hexogonal barrel gleamed in the moonlight as Hays opened the breach and slid in the long, conical cylinder that made up the bullet and casing to which the rifle had been adapted from its original ball-and-cap mechanism.

Hays was only five feet two inches tall and weighed just under 130 pounds. However, he rode a very large horse... the big black stallion standing at least two hands higher than average. The result of this unlikely combination was to make Hays look even smaller and his horse even larger than they actually were.

In the Louisiana bayou country where Hays grew up, his diminutive size had been quite a disadvantage. Strength, and the ability to use one's fists, were what established the hierarchy of the bayou. Bullied by those who were larger than he, Hays's earlier years were shadowed by intimidation and shame. Then one day, in desperation, Hays grabbed a shotgun and blew a hole in the guts of one of his tormentors.

No one else in the bayou had ever seen an argument settled by any means other than sheer strength. When they saw the strongest of their number brought down by the weakest, they were visibly frightened and they began to give Hays a new and unexpected respect. Shortly thereafter, that respect manifested itself in Hays's being elected to the position of Lieutenant in the Bayou Bengals, a regiment of Louisiana volunteers, organized to fight in the civil war.

During the war Hays discovered two things about himself. He learned that he had no compunctions about pulling the trigger, and he discovered that he liked the feeling of power he experienced by seeing others cowering before him. It was a feeling he didn't intend to surrender ever again.

While others cursed the war, Hays enjoyed it. It was as if society had created an environment just for him. He could kill as often as he wanted, and as long as the men he killed wore a different color uniform from the one he was wearing, he would be honored, instead of condemned.

It was the best thing that had ever happened to him, but when the war was over he found himself without an avocation. Then he discovered a trade that would allow him to continue to use his skill. He became a bounty hunter, specializing only in the most desperately wanted men, the "Dead or Alive" cases. This way he could kill without compunction—and without fear of punishment—while also being paid for it. It was as if the business had been developed especially for him.

When reward posters were circulated on Rollo Doran and members of his band of rustlers, Hays came to San Pedro to ply his avocation. When he made inquiries about Doran and his gang, he was told that the Cattlemen's Association had entered into an agreement with Will and Gid Crockett.

"Is the Cattlemen's Association in the habit of hiring wanted men?" Hays asked.

"Wanted men?"

Hays produced an old, yellowed poster on the Crocketts.

WANTED DEAD OR ALIVE
For Murder and Mayhem
By the State of Kansas
Will and Gid Crockett
$1,500 for Each

"Why, that circular is several years old," Hays was told.

"Don't matter none. There's no statute of limitations on murder," Hays replied.

The situation now seemed made-to-order for Hays. He could not only eliminate his competition, he could get paid for it. He made an attempt at one of the Crocketts and had missed. He planned to try again, but not just yet. He needed to back away a bit, to give the Crocketts time to let their guard down again. Hays was most deadly when the element of surprise was on his side.

Hays had a unique way of operating his business. He called it "running a trap line." By putting out the proper bait, he could reasonably expect his quarry to show up in one of his traps.

The saloon in Cochise Springs was one such trap. Hays let it be known that an accomplice was needed for an easy payroll robbery. Anyone interested in the job was to walk out of the saloon at exactly nine o'clock in the evening on this very day, come to the lamppost by the stable, and examine his pocket watch. That would be the signal by which they would meet. Further arrangements would be concluded at that time.

Earlier that day, Hays learned that someone had, indeed, taken the bait. It was Butch Campbell. Though Campbell had been a small fry up until now, he had recently killed a bank teller in a botched hold-up attempt, and was now worth $1,000, "Dead or Alive." For someone like Wilson Hays, collecting that $1,000 would be as easy as picking an apple from a tree.

Inside the saloon, Butch Campbell stood at the bar nursing a beer. He had come in with just enough money for a beer and a plate of beans. He had nearly been killed during his last robbery attempt, and hadn't gotten one red cent for his troubles. He wished he had enough money to go into the back room with one of the two women who were working the bar, but he didn't. He didn't even have enough money for a second beer.

If everything worked out though, that would soon change. Campbell was here to meet a man to plan a job. After that, his pockets would be full again. He looked over at the wall clock.

"Is your clock right?" he asked the bartender.

The bartender, who was busy polishing glasses, set the towel down and pulled out his watch. He flipped open the case and looked at it, then glanced back at the clock.

"Yes, sir," he said. "It is lacking five minutes of nine o'clock."

"Thanks," Campbell replied.

"Would you like another beer, sir?"

"No, thank you. Not just yet," Campbell answered.

"Very good, sir."

The bartender went back to wiping glasses. Campbell raised his nearly empty beer mug. There was just enough beer left to wet his lips.

According to the instructions, Campbell was to go outside and stand under the lamppost in front of the livery at exactly nine o'clock, and examine his pocket watch. He didn't actually have a pocket watch—he had sold it long ago. But he figured if he pretended to be examining one, it would amount to the same thing.

He took another swallow of beer, then made a face. He had been nursing the beer so long that it had gone flat on him. It was pure hell to be in this world without money. He looked back toward the Regulator clock and saw the minute hand move to one minute until nine. He finished his beer, slapped the mug down, wiped the back of his hand across his mouth and started for the door.

"Come again," the bartender called to him.

"When you've got more money," one of the bar girls called. She followed her chiding with a high-pitched laugh. The man with her guffawed in a rich, bass tone.

"I will," Campbell replied.

Like hell, he thought. When he had enough money, he was going to go to someplace where he could have a good time ... someplace like Denver or maybe even San Francisco. He wouldn't be caught dead in a place like this.

Outside, a waiting Hays held a match to his watch face and saw that it was five till nine. He figured that was close enough to the time that it wouldn't be necessary for him to check it anymore. All he would have to do is wait for his man to show, and that should be any time now.

A man came out of the saloon and stepped into the

street. He stood there for a moment looking in both directions. Hays raised the rifle to his shoulder and waited. The man looked back toward the saloon and shouted something, then another man came out and the two of them walked together toward the opposite end of the town, away from the stable.

Hays lowered the rifle.

Behind him his horse whickered and stamped its foot.

Somewhere down in the little town, a dog barked. A back door slammed shut in one of the houses and, in the moonlight, Hays saw a man heading for the toilet, carrying a wad of paper with him.

From the saloon he heard a woman's high-pitched laugh, then the lower guffaw of her companion.

A mule brayed.

Another patron came out of the saloon door and, like the first man, stood for a moment on the street, looking both ways. Hays watched him carefully, then saw him start toward the stable. Again, Hays raised his rifle and pointed it toward the street lamp.

The man stopped under the light of the lamp, reached into his pocket then raised his hand to study it pointedly. Hays aimed at the easy target the street lamp provided for him, squeezed the trigger slowly, then was rocked back by the recoil of the exploding cartridge. Even from here, he could see part of the man's skull fly away as the heavy lead slug crashed through his head.

The heavy boom of the shot rolled back from the distant hills so that it sounded almost like a volley, rather than one exceptionally well-placed shot. Hays mounted his horse and rode quickly toward the sprawled body of the man he had just shot. By the time he got there, more than two dozen townspeople, men, women and children, had poured out of the saloon, the closer houses and other buildings, to gather around the body.

"Who did this?" someone was asking. "Did anybody see anything?"

Hays saw a glint of light on the questioner's chest and realized that it was the reflection of a star. This was the sheriff.

"I did it, Sheriff," Hays said, swinging down from his horse.

"You?" the sheriff asked. His eyes narrowed as he took Hays in, a small man, dressed in black, riding a big black horse with a long rifle sheathed on one side, and a sawed-off shotgun on the other.

"Who the hell are you, Mister? You dry-gulch a man, then just come ridin' in here bold as life and announce you're the one that did it?" He pulled his pistol. "You're under arrest."

"I don't think so," Hays said. He pulled a poster from his shirt pocket and showed it to the sheriff. "Unless I miss my guess, this fella is Butch Campbell."

The sheriff unfolded the poster and looked at it. He read it quickly, then looked back at Hays. "What do you mean, unless you miss your guess? You mean you ain't sure?"

"Well, I was back up there on the hill," Hays said. "And of course, it being dark and all, I could be mistaken. But I don't think I am."

"My god, mister, you tryin' to tell us you took him down from way back there?"

"If you go back to that stand of cottonwood trees, you'll find the empty shell casing," Hays answered.

"My god, that's over five hundred yards away ... in the dark," someone said in awe.

"I'm goin' to get me that shell casing," a young boy shouted, and his declaration set in motion half a dozen other young boys, all scampering to be the first to lay claim to the souvenir.

"Anyone know this man?" the sheriff asked.

"It's Butch Campbell, all right," one of the men who had been drinking with him in the saloon said.

"Well, there you go, Sheriff. Looks like I got the right man after all," Campbell said. "As you can see by the dodger, there's a thousand-dollar reward out on him. Dead or alive," he added pointedly. He nodded toward the hotel. "I'm going to take a room in the hotel for tonight. I expect you'll have verification and payment by noon tomorrow, won't you?"

The sheriff nodded. "I reckon I will," he said. "But, by damn, I don't mind tellin' you, somethin' like this just doesn't sit right."

"Just have the money," Hays said.

"He sure is full of himself," one of the saloon patrons said as Hays started toward the hotel.

"Shhh!" someone said. "He might hear you."

"What do I care if he hears me? Hell, the little shit wouldn't dress out much over a hundred pounds."

"A rattlesnake isn't very big either," the sheriff pointed out. "But you don't go pissing one of them off, if you can help it."

Back in San Pedro, Will and Gid had answered a summons to come to the Chamberlain Ranch.

"What do you think?'" Chamberlain asked, pointing to the new house. "Of course, it doesn't have anything but a canvas cover for a roof, but by the time we get a roof on, it'll be as fine as the old one ever was."

"It'll be even better," Elsie said, beaming proudly. "I was hoping to get the old house fixed up, or maybe even get a new one. Of course, I never planned on getting it this way," she added.

"You got it built pretty fast," Will said.

"That's the way it is out here when neighbors get together," Chamberlain said. "Mostly it was the Association."

"Ah, yes, the Association," Will said.

"They've been pretty hard on you boys, haven't they? I apologize for that."

"Don't worry about it. It comes with the territory," Gid said.

"Nevertheless, they're coming at you two like the Spanish Inquisition or something," Chamberlain said. "They have no right to question your methods or your motives."

"I appreciate your kind words," Will said.

"Words? Humph. Words are a dime a dozen," Elsie replied. "We want you to eat dinner with us."

Gid grinned broadly. "Miz Chamberlain, I like the way you think," he said.

Dinner was fried chicken, mashed potatoes, fresh butter-beans, biscuits, and gravy. It was topped off with large slices of apple pie.

Leigh ate with them. He apologized and explained that as he was the only hand remaining, he had taken to eating with the family. Elsie said he was almost like one of the family anyway, and Will noticed in the exchange of glances between Leigh and Dottie, that he might, indeed, be a part of the family some day.

"Pa," Dottie said after the dessert was finished, "can we show him now?"

Chamberlain smiled. "Sure, I guess now's as good a time as any," he said. "Will, if you don't mind, I'd like you to come on out to the barn with us. Dottie and Leigh have something they want to show you." Chamberlain looked over at Gid. " 'Course, you can come too, Gid. But this is mostly for Will."

"Well then, if you don't mind, I think I'll just have me another piece of pie," Gid said. He looked at Elsie. "That is ... if it wouldn't be puttin' you out any," he added.

Elsie chuckled. "It so happens, Gid, that I held back the largest piece, just in case you would want seconds. Same as before? Topped with a slab of cheese?"

"Yes'm," Gid said. "That was mighty good."

As Gid started on his second piece of pie, Will followed Chamberlain and the others outside. Leigh went into the barn, then, a moment later, came back, leading a big black horse. The horse, which was already saddled, was a magnificent animal, with a coat so lustrous and black that the sunbeams that played off him danced in flashes of blue lightning.

"You'll be needin' a horse to replace the one you got killed," Chamberlain said.

"Yes," Will said. He pointed to the horse he had ridden out on. "I rented this one from the stable."

"What about this one?"

Will went over to look at the horse more closely. He

was a perfect figure of conformation with flared nostrils and eyes that flashed fire.

"You like him?" Dottie asked Will.

"He's about the best-looking piece of horse flesh I've ever seen," Will said, patting him on the neck. "How much are you asking for him?"

"He's not for sale," Chamberlain said.

"What? But I thought..."

"He's yours," Dottie said. "A gift to you from us."

"No," Will replied. "I can't do that. I can't take him for nothing."

"Sure you can," Chamberlain insisted. Elsie and Dottie and Leigh and I have already discussed it, and we figured we owe you something for what you did for us ... not only helping us fight off the raid, but also in letting us claim the reward. You got your horse killed, you need another one, and we want to give this one to you."

"He's a good one," Leigh said. "I raised him myself, from a colt. I was going to make him a part of my string, but I think you'll have better use for him."

"Get on him, see how it feels," Chamberlain suggested.

Will swung up into the saddle, then leaned down and patted the horse on the neck a couple of times.

"Go ahead," Leigh said. "Give him a run. I want you to see what you've got."

"All right," Will agreed. "I'll just do that." He slapped

his legs against the horse's sides. "Let's go," he said.

The horse burst forward like a cannonball, reaching top speed at once, surprising Will by its immediate response. Will bent low over his withers, feeling the rush of wind in his face and experiencing the pure thrill of the run, feeling almost as if he and the horse were one, sharing the same muscle structure and bloodstream. The horse's hooves drummed a rapid rhythm against the ground and it kicked up little spurts of dust behind him. Will pulled him to a stop and turned him. He was amazed at how far he had come in such a short time. As he returned to the little group in front of the barn, he had a big grin on his face.

"What do you think?" Leigh asked.

"I have to tell you, this is more horse than I've ever been on before."

"You'll take him then?" Dottie asked, anxiously.

"Miss Chamberlain, right now I believe I'd fight anyone who tried to take him away from me," Will replied as a wide grin crossed his face.

"He's yours," Chamberlain said. "Come inside and I'll give you a bill of sale."

"I've never given him a name," Leigh said. "So you can call him anything you want."

Will smiled. "He doesn't need a name. He knows who he is and I know who I am."

Chapter Fifteen

Three days later Will and Gid uncovered what they had been looking for. They found the valley where the rustlers were hiding out.

Actually, they were pretty sure of its location even before they found it, because they had already looked up every other valley and draw within thirty miles of San Pedro, and this was the only place left that it could be. Then, when they started exploring this canyon and saw that it had a narrow, easily guarded entrance, they knew they were in the right spot. After that, there was nothing left for them to do but dismount and let their horses crop grass while they sat in the shade and kept watch for a while.

It was mid-afternoon when two riders finally exited the canyon. One was tall and lanky, with a bushy, walrus-type mustache. The other was short and stocky with a scraggly beard.

"Will?" Gid said.

"Yeah, I see them."

"Ever seen 'em before?"

"They were with Bean and Townsen when they tried to hit the Holeman place," Will said.

Will and Gid moved out to a ledge which overlooked the pass, then lay very still as the two rustlers rode right beneath them. They were so close, they could hear the riders as they were talking.

"I tell you, Martin, we ought not to be doin' this. Doran ain't goin' to like it much, us ridin' out on our own," the short, stocky rider said.

"He'll calm down when we bring in a side of beef," the tall, lanky one answered. "Come on, Grinnell, admit it. Ain't you getting' damn hungry for somethin' more'n beans and tortillas? Wouldn't a little beefsteak go good now and again?"

"Yeah," Grinnell replied. "It would. But I still don't know if this is such a good idea. I mean, plannin' a job on our own."

"What job?" Martin replied. "This ain't no job. I mean, we ain't really goin' out to do any rustlin' or anything. We're goin' to find one cow, that's all. And we ain't even goin' to drive it anywhere. We're goin' to butcher it on the spot and we're goin' to bring back the choice pieces. We'll be back before sundown and have beef in our bellies before we go to sleep."

The two men continued their conversation but they rode out of ear shot so that Will and Gid were no longer able to follow what they were saying. It didn't matter. They didn't have to hear any more... they had already heard enough to realize that these two men were acting on their own, and that no one else would be coming out behind them.

Will and Gid hurried back to their horses, mounted, then rode parallel with the two riders while also making a very big circle so as not to be seen by Martin and Grinnell. They put their horses into ground-eating lopes and easily raced ahead of them. Then, a few minutes later, they suddenly appeared on the trail just ahead of the two riders. Startled by their unexpected appearance, both horses reared and Martin and Grinnell had to fight them to bring them under control.

Will and Gid sat there, calmly, patting their own horses reassuringly, so they wouldn't be spooked by the antics of Martin and Grinnell's animals.

"Good evenin' boys," Will said easily.

"Son of a bitch, it's the Crocketts! Where'd you two come from?" Grinnell shouted. Once he had his horse under control, his shoulder jerked as if he were about to go for his gun, but Will shook his head and cocked the pistol he was already holding in his hand. The metallic sound of the clicking sear as the cylinder rolled into position was cold and frightening, and it stopped Grinnell before he made a mistake. Grinnell dropped his free arm by his side.

"You two unbuckle your gun belts and hand them to my brother," Will ordered.

Grinnell and Martin took off their gun belts then handed them to Gid, who hooked both of them across his saddle pommel.

"What do you want with us?" Martin asked.

Will waved the barrel of his pistol in a motion to indicate they should get going. "I want you to come along with us," he said.

"Why should we do that?"

"Because, dead or alive, you're money in the bank for us," Gid said. "Now, go ahead, do what my brother said before you get him pissed off."

It was nearly sundown by the time Will and Gid herded their two prisoners into San Pedro. A shimmer of sunlight bounced off the roofs and sides of the buildings, painting the town red as they prodded the prisoners down the street toward the marshal's office.

Next door to the marshal's office was the Cattlemen's Association and across the street from that was the saloon. The boys were thirsty and they could almost taste the beer they would be drinking in a few minutes. Their thirst was heightened by the large sign which the saloon was touting. It was a painting of a golden mug of beer hanging out over the boardwalk, squeaking an invitation as it swung back and forth in the late-afternoon breeze.

They rode straight to the jail. Gid dismounted first, while Will kept an eye on the prisoners. Then with Gid watching them from the ground, Will dismounted.

"Get down, you two," Gid ordered.

Marshal Jackson met them just in front of the door. "Well, here's a change," Jackson said. "You brought me a couple of live ones." Jackson looked at the two prisoners. "Come on in, boys. I think you're going to like it here."

"You think you're going to keep us here, old man?" Grinnell asked. "As soon as Doran finds out where we are, he's going to come in here and take this town apart. You just mark my words."

"Is that a fact?" Jackson replied. He opened the door. "Well, then, we'd better keep you where he can find you, don't you think?"

"I'm tellin' you, old man, you're makin' a very big mistake," Grinnell said again.

"It won't be my first mistake," Jackson said. He slammed the door behind them, then turned the key in the lock.

"Maybe it ain't your first. But it could be your last," Martin said ominously.

"Where'd you find them?" Jackson asked Will as he walked over to re-hang the key on the hook on the wall.

"About ten miles from here," Will answered. "We found the place where they're all holed up. So, we just waited around outside long enough, and these two came out."

"Who are they, do you know?"

"One of them is called Martin, the other is called Grinnell. That's all I know."

"Here they are," Gid said. He had been leafing through a pile of wanted posters from the moment they stepped into the marshal's office. Now he pulled a couple of them out and showed them to Jackson.

"The tall one with the mustache is Vale Martin. The short one with the beard is L. Q. Grinnell."

"I'll get word out to Doc Stiles that you brought two more in," Jackson said. "Where will I find you?"

"After we take care of the horses you'll probably find us in the saloon," Will said.

"And if we aren't there, we'll be down to Big Sal's Place," Gid added.

"All right, I'll find you," Jackson said.

The two boys boarded their horses, as well as the two horses that belonged to the rustlers, in the livery. The sun had completely set now, and it was dark as they walked down to the bright lights of the saloon. The saloon was fairly crowded, filled with smoke and ringing with laughter and dozens of conversations. In addition to the filled tables, there were several customers standing at the bar. At a table nearest the cold stove, four men played cards.

"What'll it be?" the bartender asked.

"Beer," Gid said, answering for both of them.

The barkeep drew the beers, then put the two mugs on the bar. Gid blew some of the foam off the head, then drank his entire beer down before he lowered the mug. He set the empty stein on the bar and let out a long, satisfied sigh.

"That one was for thirst," he said. "Now I'll take one for taste."

"Be glad to," the bartender replied, refilling his mug.

Over at the card table, one of the players stood up. "Well, boys, I've enjoyed the game, but I've got to get out to the ranch. I'm ridin' night hawk."

"Nice of you to leave some of your money with us, Dan," one of the other players said, and all laughed.

"Yeah, well, I'll get it back next time." As Dan walked away, saying goodbye to the others in the saloon, he left an opening at the table.

Gid sat his mug down on the bar, empty for the second time

"Another?" the bartender asked.

"No, thanks," Gid said. He smiled. "I've enjoyed the beer, but beer's not the only thing I come back to town for. You coming, Will?"

Will, who was looking at the table with the open chair, shook his head.

"You go ahead, Gid. I think I'll play a little cards."

Gid snorted. "I like a game of cards as much as the next fella," he said. "But I have to tell you, playing cards ain't what I've been thinkin' about these last several days out on the range."

Annie gave a squeal of delight when she saw Gid coming through the front door. She ran to him and threw her arms around him.

"Oh, I've been wondering when you would come back," she said.

"Have you missed me?"

"Have I missed you?" She grabbed his hand, then began to pull on him as she started toward the stairs.

"What are you doing?" Gid asked.

"I'm going to show you how much I missed you," Annie replied.

"Don't you want to visit a little?"

"We can visit later," Annie insisted.

Annie took Gid upstairs, then into her room. When the door was closed behind them the piano music and the laughter from the downstairs salon faded quickly into the background. The effect was sudden and dramatic. It was as if they had been magically transported to another time and place so that they were, truly, alone.

Annie leaned over and extinguished the lantern, but the moon outside was high and so full and bright that even without the lamp, the room was still illuminated by a soft light. It cast everything in subtle shadows of silver and black, allowing them to see each other as they began to remove their clothes.

At the card table, Will tried to complete a spade flush, but he drew a heart instead. With a little groan, he lay his cards down.

One of the other players chuckled. "Didn't get what you were after, eh?"

"Afraid not," Will said.

"Say," one of the other players said. "Did you fellas hear about what happened over to Cochise Springs?"

"No, what happened over there? Did they catch the preacher in bed with the mayor's wife, or somethin'?"

Everyone, including Will, laughed.

"No sir. A fella named Butch Campbell got hisself killed."

"That ain't much news," one of the other players snorted. "The way things is goin' around here, we're gettin' someone killed just about ever' day."

The man suddenly realized that he was sitting at a

table with one of the men responsible for most of the killings, and he blanched, visibly, then reached for his beer to try and cover his embarrassment by taking a drink. "I... I'm sorry, Mr. Crockett," he mumbled. "I didn't mean nothin' by that remark."

"That's all right, Mister," Will said easily. "My brother and I have done a lot of killing. Only thing I can say is, we haven't killed anyone who wasn't trying to kill us."

"Yeah, well, that wasn't the case with this fella over in Cochise Springs," the first man said, trying to recapture the attention. "This fella, Campbell, was just standing there under a streetlamp. He was killed by a rifle shot from five hundred yards away. In the dark."

"What? You trying to tell us someone made a five-hundred-yard rifle shot—in the dark?"

"Yep. He was shooting one of those Whitworth rifles, you know, the kind the sharpshooters used during the war."

That bit of information got Will's attention and he looked over at the speaker.

"Did they get who did it?" he asked.

"Weren't no gettin' to it. It was all legal. Turns out the fella who did the shootin' was a bounty hunter. Campbell was a wanted man, dead or alive."

"Wanted or not, there's nothing sporting about shooting a man from concealment in the dark."

"Well, I agree with you," the storyteller said. "Still in all, you got to hand it to ole' Hays. That was one hell of a shot."

"Hays?" Will asked.

"Wilson Hays. Like I say, he's a bounty hunter. You ever run across him?"

"I damn near did," Will replied. He was convinced, now that Wilson Hays was the mysterious shooter who had killed his horse, and nearly killed him.

Chapter Sixteen

The cards weren't falling well, so bidding goodbye to the other players around the table, Will quit the game. He walked on through the bar then stepped out onto the front porch for some fresh air. That was when someone came running up to him, out of breath and clearly excited about something.

"Say, aren't you one of them fellas that brought in them two rustlers today?"

"Yes."

"Iffen you don't want them to get away, you'd best get on down to the livery right away," the man said.

"Why? What's happening?"

"While the marshal was out makin' his rounds, them two prisoners got the jump on the boy that comes around ever' night to clean up the jail. Jackson seen 'em just as they was gettin' away and he's got 'em holed up in the livery. The only thing is, they killed that clean-up boy so they say they ain't got nothin' to lose now, and they ain't goin' to give up. They say they're goin' to kill the livery boy if the marshal don't let 'em go."

"Thanks," Will said. He started down the street toward the livery and saw that there were already a dozen or more people gathered around the livery stable to watch the drama unfold. He noticed, also, that none of them were offering to help the marshal. He looked around for Jackson, but didn't see him anywhere.

"Where's the marshal?" he asked one of the men in the crowd.

"He's in there," the man said, pointing to the livery barn.

"Inside?"

"Yeah. He yelled out a moment ago that he was goin' to come in after them two if they didn't come out with their hands up. When they didn't come out, why the marshal went on inside."

"That seems like a dumb fool thing to do," Will said. Despite his comment, he couldn't help but feel that his earlier scorn for the marshal may have been misplaced.

Will would like to have had Gid with him. The two brothers worked so well as a team that they didn't even have to speak ... each of them knew, instinctively, what the other would do. But Gid wasn't here and there was no time to wait for him. If he didn't act quickly, the marshal, and perhaps the stable boy, might be killed.

Pulling his pistol, he started toward the livery. He was almost there when he heard a muffled gunshot from the dark. He broke out into a run and had just reached the edge of the livery when he saw Jackson coming out of the shadows toward him.

"Jackson? Jackson, what is it? What's going on?" Will called. "I heard a shot."

"I'm killed, Crockett," Jackson said with a half smile on his face. He fell face down to the ground and Will ran over to him then rolled him over.

"Marshal?" Will called, but there was no answer. Jackson was right. He had been killed.

"There goes one of 'em, Crockett!" a man suddenly shouted from the other side of the livery. Will drew his pistol and stared out into the empty darkness.

A figure suddenly appeared near the corner of the livery barn. He was tall and lanky and in the ambient light, Will could see the walrus-type mustache. This was Martin.

"Give it up, Martin!" Will called.

In answer, Martin pointed his pistol toward Will and it boomed three times. In the light of the muzzle-flash, Will could see the wild, desperate features of his face.

Will shot back, only once, but once was enough. His bullet found its mark and Martin threw up his gun and fell over backward. Will ran over to the fallen outlaw and knelt beside him. He could see bubbles of blood coming from Martin's mouth. He was trying hard to breathe, and Will heard a sucking sound in his chest. He knew that his bullet had punctured Martin's lung.

"Why didn't you give it up when I called to you?" Will asked

"I figure this beats hangin'," Martin gasped.

"What about it, Mister? Is he dead?" someone asked from behind Will.

"He soon will be," Will answered. He saw the towns-people beginning to stream across the street, drawn by morbid curiosity, anxious to get a look at the bodies of Marshal Jackson and Vale Martin.

"Look at that," someone said, pointing to Martin. "He got him dead center with one shot."

Frustrated by the gathering crowd, Will stood up and waved at them. "Listen to me. You folks better get back if you don't want to get shot," he called. "There's still one left in the barn."

Almost as if in punctuation to Will's statement, there was a flash of light, then the crash of gunfire as someone fired from inside the livery. Though the bullet didn't hit anyone, it whistled so close over the heads of those in the crowd that it had the effect that Will's warning did not. With a little shout of fear, everyone turned and ran to get out of the way of the line of fire.

"He's still in there!" someone said, repeating Will's warning.

"The damned fool tried to shoot us," another said. The crowd, still unwilling to miss the show, stayed in close proximity. Now, however, they prudently found shelter behind the corners of adjacent buildings, or behind the nearby watering troughs.

"Grinnell! Grinnell, give it up," Will called into the livery.

"Now why would I want to do that?" Grinnell called back.

"Because there's only one of two ways you are going to come out of there. Either with your hands up, or dead."

"I ain't givin' up."

"Then you're coming out dead," Will warned.

"I don't think so. I've got an edge, Crockett."

"You've got nothing."

"I've got the stable boy," Grinnell called. He giggled.

"So what?"

"So what? If you try and come in here, I'm goin' to kill him, that's so what." Grinnell giggled again, confident of his bargaining position.

"Hell, that boy doesn't mean anything to me. Go ahead and kill him," Will called back. He could hear the towns-people gasping around him.

"What? What do you mean kill him?"

"I mean just what I said," Will replied. "Kill him and get it over with. Then there will just be the two of us."

"You're runnin' a bluff. You think I won't kill him?"

"Look, kill him or don't kill him," Will said. "I don't care which you do. Just shut up about it."

"You're ... you're crazy. You know that?"

"Maybe," Will said. "But I'm not the one trapped in a livery."

"Is Martin dead?"

"Yes."

"It was him killed the marshal. Not me," Grinnell said. "All I wanted to do was to get out of here."

"Is the stable boy still alive?" Will asked.

"Yes."

"Can he testify that Martin is the one who shot the marshal?"

"Yeah, he seen it."

"Send him out."

"No. He's the only chance I have. If I come out, he's going to be standing in front of me."

"Look, I'll make this easy for both of us. Have the stable boy stand in the door and I'll kill him myself. We can just get him out of the way now," Will said.

"No, wait, wait!" Grinnell called. "Maybe we can make a deal."

"What kind of deal?"

"I don't want to hang. I didn't kill the marshal."

"Well, you could always let the stable boy go. That way he could testify, and it might make you look good for the jury."

"All right," Grinnell called from the darkened interior. "All right, I'm comin' out now. I'm sending the stable boy out first. Don't shoot him."

"Go ahead."

The door to the livery opened and the stable boy stuck his head out, tentatively, then ran from the barn.

"He's out," Will said. "Now it's your turn."

"Don't shoot."

"Come out with your hands up," Will said. "I won't shoot."

Grinnell, like the stable boy before him, stuck his head around the edge of the door and searched anxiously up and down the street. He tossed his pistol out into the dirt.

"There," he called. "I ain't armed."

"Get your hands up and come on out."

Grinnell stepped outside. Then, with his hands in the air, he started toward Will. He took only three steps when, from one of the darkened buildings back in the town, a rifle barked. Grinnell crumpled and went down.

"Who fired that shot?" Will yelled over his shoulder. "Who fired?"

No one answered and Will hurried over to Grinnell's crumpled body.

"I thought you said you wouldn't shoot," Grinnell coughed.

"I didn't," Will answered. "I don't know who did it."

Grinnell tried to laugh, but a spasm of coughing overtook him instead. "Why did he shoot me?" he asked. "I wasn't goin' to say anything."

"Why did who shoot you?"

Grinnell's breath came in a series of raspy gasps.

"Grinnell, who do you think shot you?"

The raspy gasps stopped and Will put his hand to Grinnell's neck. He was dead.

Once again the townspeople began to press forward. This time there was no one remaining to threaten their safety so that, within a few moments, the crowd around the three bodies had grown quite large.

"Well, Mr. Crockett," Doc Stiles said. "I got word from Marshal Jackson that you had brought in two live rustlers. Only by the time I got here, I learned that he was mistaken. Your prisoners are dead, and so is the marshal."

"Yeah," Will said.

"Death does seem to follow you, doesn't it?"

"I reckon it does."

Stiles sighed. "Well, there's no sense in belaboring the issue any longer. I have twice brought it to a vote to have you dismissed, and I have been defeated both times. If the Association wants to keep you on, to include your rather severe brand of justice, then I feel it is no longer my place to challenge you. Stop by tomorrow morning at seven o'clock. I'll have your money ready for you."

"Say, Mister," the stable boy said, coming up to Will. "Would you really have killed me to get at him?" He nodded toward Grinnell's body.

"Did you believe that?" Will asked.

"You're damned right I believed it," the stable boy replied.

"Then Grinnell probably believed it too," Will said. "It took away his edge."

"But would you really have done it?"

Will smiled. "If I told you, it would take away my edge," he said.

"Damn!" Doran said when he heard the news of what happened to Martin and Grinnell. "The Crocketts again. I'm tellin' you, if we don't get rid of them, they're going to get rid of us."

"Yeah, well, it ain't like we ain't been trying. They take a lot of killin', that's all."

"Bullshit. They don't take no more killin' than anyone else," Doran said. "We just got to be a little smarter with it, that's all."

When Will and Gid dropped by the office of the Cattlemen's Association at seven the next morning, they learned that, once more, Doc Stiles had called a special meeting. Several of the ranchers' horses were already tied up at the hitching rail, a couple of buggies were parked on the street, and Holeman and Woods were just arriving.

"I heard about the little fracas last night," Woods said. "Congratulations on doin' a good job."

"Thanks," Will said. He took in all the other horses with a sweep of his hand. "What's going on? Is there a meeting this morning?"

"Yes," Woods answered. "After Jackson got himself killed last night, Doc Stiles sent word out to all of us, asking us to be here at seven this morning. You mean you don't know anything about it?"

"No," Will answered.

"Say, where's Chamberlain?" Holeman asked.

"I imagine he'll be along," Woods said. Woods chuckled. "Until this meeting was called, there were several of us going to go over there and help him finish roofing his house, remember?"

"Yeah," Holeman laughed. "I don't reckon he'll want to tackle that job with just him and Leigh."

The other ranchers were already sitting around the meeting table when Will, Woods, and Holeman went inside. Stiles was at the head of the table and, with an expansive gesture, he invited them to sit down.

"Gentlemen, what do you say we get the meeting started?" Stiles began.

"Wait a minute. What about Chamberlain? He ain't here yet."

"Chamberlain won't be here, I'm afraid. He sent word that he wasn't going to be able to come. He has to run over to Pantano today." Stiles held up a piece of paper. "However, he gave me authorization to vote his proxy, if nobody protests."

"That's all right by me," Holeman said. "What about the rest of you?"

"I got no problems," one of the others said. "Woods?"

"I guess it's all right. But what's this meeting about, anyway?"

"A couple of things," Stiles said. He looked over at the Crocketts. "To begin with, Mr. Crockett, Mr. Crockett, I've been pretty hard on the two of you, lately, and I want to apologize," he said. "Several of the good people of this town have told me what happened last night and, under the circumstances, there was nothing else you could do." He slid an envelope across the table toward them. "Your money is in this envelope and I want to go on record here and now, as saying that you have my complete confidence. In fact, I would like to show that confidence by offering you a position. As you know, we are now in need of a town marshal. I'm prepared to offer the job of marshal and deputy marshal to the two of you."

"Thanks for the offer," Will said, taking the envelope. "But we aren't interested."

Stiles nodded. "I didn't really think you would be. Nor should you be, actually. The truth is, you are much more effective the way you are. However, I thought it only right that the position be offered to the two of you, or, either of you for that matter, before we offered it to anyone else." He looked at the others around the table. "However, gentlemen, his refusal does leave us with a problem. We have to have a new marshal and I'm asking for any suggestions."

"What about you, Doc?" one of the other ranchers proposed.

"Me? No, I don't see myself as marshal."

"Wait a minute, why not?" Woods asked. "You're the head of the Cattlemen's Association. You could combine the two jobs."

"Gentlemen, you forget I have a ranch to run. A larger ranch, I might add, than any of you."

"Well, yes, but you've found the time to be president of the Cattlemen's Association. You can find time to do this as well. It needs doin', Doc, you can't get around that."

"But being a marshal is a full-time job."

"It don't have to be. I mean, you've got a foreman to help with the ranch, and you can appoint as many deputies as you want to help with the marshaling," one of the other men said. "Come on, Doc, we're not sayin' you have to make night rounds like Jackson did. Just sort of be over things.

"Like a general," another suggested.

"A general," Stiles said. He smiled. "Well, as someone who never got any higher than private in the war, I must confess that I like the sound of that." He drummed his fingers on the table for a while, then he nodded his head. "All right," he said. "I am committed to running the rustlers out and bringing peace to the valley. And if the only way to do that is to be your marshal, then I'll be your marshal. But only until this business is all taken care of. After that, like a general after a war is over, I intend to go back to being a private citizen and a rancher. I hope, a prosperous rancher."

The others laughed, then there was a spattering of applause around the table. Stiles looked over at Will and Gid.

"Gentlemen, now that I am officially the marshal I'll say the same thing I said a few moments ago as a rancher and as the head of the Cattlemen's Association. I appreciate, that is, we all appreciate the job you've been doing and you have my full and complete support."

"Thanks," Will said again. He and Gid stood up. "Now, if you men will excuse us, we're going to get a little breakfast, then go back to work."

"Good luck," Stiles called to them. "Now, gentlemen, I want to talk about the price per head at the cattle pens in Kansas City. I think we can ..." That was as far as Stiles got before Will and Gid left the office. Then they walked across the street to the Monterey Cafe.

Although Gid, of the two brothers, was known as the biggest eater, on this morning Will more than held his own. Breakfast consisted of a stack of pancakes, two eggs, fried potatoes, an oversized piece of ham, and half a dozen biscuits each. They were just washing it all down with a second cup of coffee when an old Mexican woman came into the cafe, looked around until she saw them, then shuffled over to their table.

"You are the Senors Crockett?" she asked.

"Yes."

"This is for you." She handed him a note.

> *Crockett,*
>
> *We have the Chamberlain girl.*
>
> *Doran*

"Wait!" Will called, standing up quickly. The woman stopped. "Where did you get this?"

"A man gave it to me," she answered. "He gave me money to give it to you."

"What man?' Will asked. He had given the note to Gid who, by now, had read it as well.

"I do not know him, Senor. I do laundry at the edge of town. He rode in, gave me the note, then rode away."

"Thanks," Will said. He took the note back from Gid and looked at it again, then, with a sigh of frustration, put it in his pocket.

"We've got to go after her," Will said.

"You'll get no argument from me, Big Brother," Gid said. "But you know what you always say."

"Yeah, I know. But we're going after her," Will said again.

Will knew what Gid was talking about. They were now faced with the very situation they were always trying to avoid. Because of the kind of life they led, they made it a practice never to establish relationships with anyone, male or female. This wasn't because of any particular antisocial behavior on their part; this was based upon a very sound principle. They knew they could always be responsible for themselves, but they couldn't always be responsible for anyone else. That wasn't a very healthy situation, for if they were close to anyone, an enemy could get to them through that person. On the other hand if they were close to no one, an enemy would have no way to get to them. In this way they were able to deny any potential enemy an "edge."

For the most part, the theory worked well. Sometimes, however, there were those borderline cases where one or both of them might be vulnerable. Dottie Chamberlain was just such a case. Though no official relationship had been established between Will and Dottie Chamberlain, their paths had crossed frequently enough that Will could no longer regard her with total detachment. Even the horse he was riding now had been a gift from Dottie Chamberlain and her father. If Doran did have her, Will knew that he had no choice. He would have to go after her.

Doran had found his edge. Will didn't like it much when the other fellow had an edge.

Chapter Seventeen

At first it was just a thin wisp, like nothing more than a column of dust in the distance. But as the Crocketts drew closer to the Chamberlain Ranch, the wisp of dust took on more substance until it became a column of smoke, growing thicker and heavier until finally it was a heavy, black cloud, filled with glowing embers and roiling into the sky.

This was Doran's second visit to the ranch and, like before, he had left fire and smoke as his calling cards. Once again, Doran was burning them out.

The fire was still snapping and popping when Will and Gid arrived but there was little left to burn. The new house, so recently built to replace the one that had been burned out before, was now a twisted mass of blackened timbers with just enough fuel left to support the dying flames.

Doran had been more thorough this time than he had been before, because this time the barn, smokehouse, and grainery were also in flames. In addition to the fires there had been a wanton slaughter of all the farm animals. Two dray-horses lay dead in the corral, half a dozen pigs were slaughtered, and there were even a handful of dead chickens scattered about.

Will saw Chamberlain then, face down in a pool of his own blood. When he went over to get a closer look at the rancher, he saw that the older man had been shot several times in the head and chest. He knew, even before he reached him, that Chamberlain was dead. Elsie, also dead, was lying nearby, at his side in death as she had been in life.

"Crockett? Crockett, is that you?" The voice that called was strained with pain and when Will looked toward it, he saw Leigh on the ground over near the watering trough. He hurried over to him. "We sure could've used your gun this time, partner," Leigh said.

"When did this happen?" Will asked.

"This mornin', just after daylight," Leigh answered. "We sure wasn't expectin' nothin' like this. They wasn't here to steal nothin'. They just come out here to murder and to burn. They went plumb crazy. After they shot me an' Mr. and Mrs. Chamberlain, they commenced to killin' all the animals. No reason for it, they didn't take no meat nor nothin', they just killed and killed and killed. By then there wasn't nothin' left I could do, so I just lay over here real still and pretended to be dead."

He sat up and Will saw that he had at least three bullet holes in him, two in the thigh and one in the arm. They were painful and he had lost a lot of blood, but he would probably live.

"Who did this, Leigh? Was it Doran?"

"Yeah, it was Doran. Him and about eight others," Leigh said. "I got two of 'em. You'll find 'em over there, both dead. But there's at least six, maybe seven of 'em left."

"You did all you could do," Will said.

Suddenly Leigh reached up and grabbed Will's arm and squeezed it tight, as if just remembering something that was important. "They got Dottie, Crockett. They got Dottie and they took her off with them. She was callin' for me to help her but I... I couldn't do nothin' for her. Go after her, Crockett. Get her back from those bastards."

"They're using her as bait," Will said. "They took her to get us to come after them."

"Well, hell, you are goin' after her, ain't you?"

"I don't know," Will said. "I do know that that is what they want us to do."

Leigh raised his gun and pointed it at Will, though he had such little strength to keep it up, that the barrel weaved around in tiny circles.

"Damnit, man," Leigh said. "Didn't you hear what I said? They got Dottie! Now, tell me you're going to bring her back safe, or so help me God I'll shoot you myself."

"Is that what you want to do, Leigh?" Will asked, easily.

Leigh lowered the gun and shook his head.

"Don't worry, we're going after her," Will said easily. "And we'll bring her back, I promise."

"I'm goin' to hold you to that, Crockett," Leigh said. "I can't go myself, so you two boys are the only chance she's got."

"We'll get her," Will promised, hating the fact that he had let himself get so involved, yet determined to follow through with his promise.

"Thanks," Leigh said. He smiled broadly. "I knew I could count on you boys." He held his gun up and looked at it, then smiled. "Couldn't of shot you anyway," he said. "I already used up all the bullets. That's why I had to just lie here an' watch helplessly."

"Which way did they go, Leigh?" Gid asked.

"South."

"South?" That surprised Will. He and Gid had located the hideout, and it was north of the ranch. However, they might have known by now that they had been found. If so, they would have to go someplace else.

"Crockett. Dottie's wearin' a red dress. You ought to be able to spot that a mile away."

"Thanks."

"Bring her back to me, Crockett. There's somethin' I haven't ever got aroun' to tellin' her yet."

Dottie sat on her horse looking at Doran and the others who had come to kill her ma and pa and Leigh, then burn her ranch. Doran was holding his hat in his hand, wiping his hairless brow with a bandanna. He looked back at Dottie and laughed a greasy, evil-sounding laugh.

"How are you doin' little lady? Are you holdin' up all right?"

"I find it hard to believe that you are actually concerned about my comfort," Dottie replied sarcastically.

"Yeah, sure," Doran said. "After all, I want to be a good host." He laughed at his own joke.

"Why did you kill all the others but take me?"

"Why do you care? You're alive, ain't you? Ain't that all that's important?"

"No. There are some things that are more important than merely being alive."

"Yeah? Well, maybe for folks like you, folks who are noble and all that. But I ain't noble. Tell me about the Crocketts."

"What?" Dottie asked, surprised by the question. "Will and Gid Crockett. Tell me about them."

"What do you want to know? They're good men."

"Will they come for you?"

"Will they come for me? I don't know. Why should they come for me?"

"Because I sent them a note tellin' them I had you," Doran said.

Dottie looked surprised. "You told them where I was? Why would you do that?"

"Don't you understand anything at all? I'm usin' you, girlie. I'm usin' you as bait."

Doran pulled his pistol and turned the cylinder to check the loads, then he put the pistol back in his holster.

"You did all this just to get the Crocketts to come after you?" Dottie asked. "You're mad! They have been after you all along. That's the whole reason they're here."

"Yeah, well, I want them on my own terms," Doran said. "From what I hear, they aren't the kind of men you mess with. I've always heard that Will Crockett was the fastest one with a gun ... but nobody ever' told me how fast Gid was. I hear that when he gunned down Aubrey Stiles, he was fast as greased lightnin'." Doran pulled his lips tight across his teeth in what might have been a smile. "That must mean Will is even faster'n greased lightnin'."

"If they are as good as all that, why would you even want them coming after you?" Dottie asked. "Aren't you afraid they might kill you?"

217

"I figure on tippin' the odds in my favor a bit," Doran. said. "Then, after I kill 'em, I'll be known all over as the man who got the Crockett brothers."

Ahead of Will and Gid, the brown land lay in empty folds of rocks, dirt and cactus. The sun heated the ground then sent up undulating waves which caused near objects to shimmer, and nonexistent lakes to appear tantalizingly in the distance. Gid picked up the tracks, but the ground was hard and the signs so indistinct that he couldn't tell very much about them. He didn't know if Dottie was one of the riders or not.

"You're the tracker, Little Brother," Will said. "What do you think?"

"All I can do is go with what my gut tells me," Gid said. "And my gut tells me we're on the right track."

Half an hour later, Gid's gut instinct was proven correct when a pistol bullet fried the air between them.

"Will!"

"I'm all right!" Will answered. "Where is he? Do you see him?"

"No!"

Both brothers dismounted, then slapped the flanks of their horses to send them out of danger. As they dived behind a nearby rock outcropping, the would-be assailant fired again. The bullet ricocheted off a rock very near

Will, sending shreds of hot lead into his face before it whined away from him.

The hidden gunman laughed. "Pretty close, wasn't I? Did that sting a little?"

"Where's the girl?" Will called.

"The girl? She's with Doran and the others," the voice answered.

"They leave you behind for the dirty work?"

"No. I volunteered to stay behind. You see, we've got us a pretty good pot built up for whoever kills you. I reckon that's goin' to be me."

"I doubt it. You've already missed your chance."

"They say both you boys are pretty good," the gunmen called. "How good are you?"

"Good enough to stay alive," Will called back. He motioned to Gid to move to another position so they wouldn't be bunched together and, nodding, Gid complied.

"Well I don't think just being good counts for much. I think the only thing that counts is a measure of guts. And I got that. The name's Gray. Heber Gray. You ever heard of me?"

"Can't say as I have," Will answered.

"Yeah? Well, after I kill both of you, I reckon folks will know who I am."

"You aren't afraid of us, Gray?"

"Naw, I ain't afraid. The way I've heard it, you two boys

do most of your shootin' in the back, or against blowhards like Aubrey Stiles. He was a blowhard, you know."

"I'd say you called it about right," Will replied. "Aubrey Stiles was pretty much of a blowhard." He moved around, trying to get into position to see his assailant.

"Say, Crockett, how'd you like it if we was to both put our guns in our holsters then step out into the open, just to see how things would come out?"

"There are two of us. Which one of us do you want?"

"I don't care which one of you I face, as long as the other one stands up in plain sight. I don't want to be shot in the back."

"Are you that brave?" Will asked.

"Well, I sure ain't goin' to piss in my pants just 'cause you say boo. I believe I can take either one of you. What do you say we try it?"

Will looked around the rock and saw that Gray was coming from behind his cover with his pistol holstered and his hands spread out beside him.

"Come on, Mr. Crockett. I'm already out here."

Will nodded at Gid, who, by now, had nearly flanked the gunman's position, and both of them stood up. The gunman seemed surprised to see that Will and Gid had managed to get that much separation between them.

Will and Gid both holstered their pistols. "I didn't really think you'd do it."

"Well, I'm a surprising man," Gray said with an evil grin. "Now!" he suddenly shouted.

Two shots went off, one from Will's immediate right, and another from behind the rock where Gray had been. One shot was aimed for Will, the other for Gid. Both bullets missed, though Will didn't know how the one that was aimed at him could have, because he was so close to the shooter that he felt the sting of burnt gunpowder.

"You dumb bastards! You missed! Both of you!" Gray shouted as he went for his own gun.

Will had a fifth of a second to make a decision. Should he fire at Heber Gray who was just now going for his gun, or should he shoot at a gunman who was now rising up from behind a nearby rock with his gun already in his hand?

Gid had no such decision to make. He picked out the one who shot at him, and was returning fire. Will decided to take on Gray. The gunman nearest him had already demonstrated his poor marksmanship in the missed shot, whereas Gray had come much closer on his first shot.

Even as he was thinking about it, Will's gun was cocked and booming. The bullet slammed into Gray's chest, severing arteries and tearing away heart tissue. Gray was dead before he hit the ground, and even before he fell, Will was already turning to fire at the other gunman. The gunman's second shot proved as ineffective as his first, but Will's bullet hit the man in the hip, causing him to double over, then crumple down in pain.

At the same time, another body came sliding, head-down, from the rocks, the victim of Gid's well placed shot.

The sound of the shooting echoed and re-echoed, as if the ghosts of the men Will and Gid had just killed were continuing the battle. When the last echo was a subdued rumble off a distant hill, the silence of the desert returned. The limbs of a nearby ocotillo rattled dryly in the breeze. A lizard scurried across a rock.

"Oh," the wounded gunman moaned. "Oh, shit, it hurts. I ain't never had nothin' to hurt like this."

"Are there any others around?" Will asked. Neither he nor Gid had holstered their pistols. Both men were looking toward the rocks and crevices for any sign of yet another hidden assailant.

"No, there was just the three of us," the gunman said through teeth, clenched in pain. "Gray said it would be easy."

"Nothing is easy," Will said, putting his gun away. "Where is the Chamberlain girl?"

"I'm gut-shot," the gunman said.

Gid knelt beside him, and looked at the bullet hole. It was in the hip, painful, but not fatal.

"My brother must be losing his touch. You aren't gut-shot," Gid said.

"I'm goin' to die."

"No you won't. Not unless I kill you," Will said. "And I will, if you don't tell me where Doran and the girl are."

"I can't tell you that. Doran will kill me if I tell you."

"I'll kill you if you don't."

The wounded gunman shook his head no.

"If that's the way you want it," Will said easily. He pointed his pistol at the wounded gunman's head.

"Wait, Will, you got to kill the last one who didn't talk," Gid said. "Let me kill this one."

"All right, Little Brother, be my guest," Will invited.

Gid cocked his pistol. The cylinder turned with a metallic click, lining up the next cartridge under the hammer and firing pin. The knuckle of his trigger finger whitened.

"No!" the gunman screamed, covering his head with his arms. "No, don't kill me!"

"Where's the girl?" Will asked again.

"This ambush wasn't my idea," the gunman said. "It wasn't even Gray's. It was Doran's. He told Gray he'd double the pot if him and me and Lewis would stay back and take care of you."

"One last time. Where is the girl?"

"All I know is they was headed for a little Mex town called San Lazeto."

"Give me your gun," Will said.

"What?"

"I said give me your gun."

"Look here, Crockett. You ain't goin' to leave me out here unarmed, are you? They might be Indians around. Snakes, wolves, all sorts of things."

"We're doin' you a favor," Will said. "The way you shoot, you're likely to shoot yourself."

Will took the gun from Gray's hand. Gid went over to the other gunman's bodies, and took their guns as well.

"Where are your horses?"

"Right over there, behind them rocks," the wounded gunman answered, pointing off to his left.

Will walked over and retrieved the three horses. He shoved the pistols into the saddle bag of one of the animals.

"Take off your boots," Will ordered.

The gunman did as he was instructed and Will put the boots in the stirrups, then slapped the horses on the flanks, sending them running.

"Wait a minute! You're leavin' me out here with no gun, no horse, no water, and no boots," Beaty complained. "You can't do that! I'll die!"

"There's a town about six miles that way," Will said, pointing off to the southeast. "If you start now, you can make it there. If you try to go anywhere else, you will die. You better get goin'. The longer you stay out here, the thirstier you're goin' to get."

"I'll get you for this, Crockett," the wounded gunman said. "I'll get both of you. One of these days I'll run across you two again, and when I do, I'll get you."

"Yeah, keep thinking about that," Will suggested. "It'll keep you going."

The wounded gunman started toward the southeast, his progress impeded not only by his lack of boots, but also by the fact that he was carrying a bullet in his hip. Will watched until Gid came back with their horses. Then the two brothers swung into the saddle and rode south, heading toward San Lazeto.

Chapter Eighteen

San Lazeto was no different from any of the other Mexican towns scattered throughout the Southwest. The Mexican flavor dictated its layout... a dozen or more adobe buildings scattered around a large square. This village did happen to have a church though, a large mission which stood guard at the east end of town. The shadow of the cross fell across the churchyard as Will and Gid rode up. The padre was drawing water from a well and the two brothers dismounted and walked toward him. The priest wore a brown cassock, held together with a strip of black rawhide, from which dangled an oversized wooden crucifix. A bald spot shined from the top of the priest's head. The hair around the bald spot was gray.

"Padre," Will said, nodding at the priest.

The priest nodded back, studying the two men closely.

"We'd be obliged for a drink," Will said. "The water

in our canteens has grown a little stale." Will pulled out a couple of bills and handed them to the priest.

"This is God's water," the priest said, waving the money away. "It's free."

"The money isn't for His water, it's for His church," Will said, nodding toward the building.

The priest smiled. "Si, gracias. Bless you, my sons, bless you," he said, taking the money.

Will plunged the dipper into the bucket and scooped up the water, then drank long and deep. Gid didn't wait for the dipper, but just turned the bucket up and drank from it. The water was cool and delicious, and they drank until their bellies were full.

"Would you like to fill your canteens?" the priest offered.

"Yes, thank you," Gid said. He walked over to the horses and got both his and Will's canteens, poured out the old water, then began refilling them with fresh water, pouring it from the dipper.

"Padre, we're looking for some men who may have come in here. I'm not sure how many. Four or five of them, I would guess. And one girl. The girl with them would be young and pretty. Also, she would be wearing a red dress."

"There are five men," the priest replied. "Are they friends of yours?"

"No, I wouldn't call them friends."

"I did not think so," the priest replied. The priest studied Will and Gid for a long moment. Will felt strange, as if the priest's eyes could penetrate to his very soul. Under the priest's gaze he was stripped naked with all his past sins, actual and conceived, bared. "I am confused," the priest finally said.

"What has you confused?"

"You two have come to kill these men. This I know, for there is death in the eyes of both of you. I see also, that you are men who have killed many times, but I do not see pleasure in the killing."

"Padre, the men we seek are very evil," Will said. "They have killed many times, and they do kill for pleasure. They killed the girl's mother and father, and all those who worked on the girl's ranch."

"If I tell you and you kill them, I will be a party to it," the priest said. "I do not wish to help you kill the men."

"I think when they are through with the girl, they will kill her. If you do not wish to help us kill these men, then consider that you are helping us save the girl."

"Si. Si, I will help the girl," the padre said. "Very well, the men you are seeking, five men and a girl, rode into town early today. Then, a bit later, four men and the girl rode out."

"Only four rode out? Then that means one of the men is still here?"

228

"Si."

"What does he look like?"

"This I cannot tell you," the priest said. "I did not see any of them closely."

"Thank you," Will said. "You have been a big help."

"I will pray for the safety of the girl, Senor," the priest said.

Gid took the horses to the stable, not to board them, but to see to it that they were fed and watered. If the chase was to continue, their horses would have to be refreshed. As Gid led the horses into the stable, he saw his brother crossing the street, heading for the cantina.

The entrance to the cantina was protected, not by bat-wing doors as was routine in the more Americanized towns, but by several strings of beads. Will stood on the porch just outside the cantina for a long moment, just listening to the sounds from inside. Someone was strumming a guitar, but that didn't stop the flow of conversation. The words were Spanish mostly, though he heard a few English-speaking voices. The beads clacked against each other as Will pushed through.

Pulling his hat brim low, he stepped up to the end of the bar then looked through the place. There were more than three dozen men and women in here. Several were standing at the bar, many others were sitting around the tables. One Mexican was in a chair against the wall, holding a pretty girl, obviously one of the bar-girls, on his lap.

There were only four Americans in the bar. Figuring that his man had to be one of the four, he studied them closely. Even as he studied them though, he realized that the cantina had a few rooms in the back to be used by the whores, or putas, as the Mexicans called the women of the trade. It was possible that his man could be back there. He slapped the bar.

"Si?" the bartender asked, sliding down the bar to stand before him.

"Beer."

"We have only tequila."

"All right, tequila," Will said, putting his coin on the bar.

The bartender filled a glass and Will took a drink, screwing his face up against its controlled fire.

One of the Americans laughed. "What's the matter, Mister? You don't like Mexican Mule Piss?" he asked. The others laughed with him.

"Sure," Will answered. "I like it just fine."

"Say, why don't you come over here and join us in a friendly game of cards?" one of the other cowboys called. "We don't get too many Americans through here."

"Yeah," the first one said. "There's just the four of us and we get tired of looking at each other's ugly mugs every day."

Will took his drink over to the table and sat down to join them. "You mean all four of you live here."

"Yeah. I'm Slim, that's Pork, he's Dirk and that's Scrub. We cowboy for Senor Gomez. Ain't that somethin' though? I mean a bunch of American's workin' for a Mexican."

"Gomez is Mex, all right, but he's fair and he pays good wages," Pork said.

"Yeah," Slim agreed. "He's a good man. Don't get us wrong, we ain't apologizin' for workin' for him or nothin'. Just remarkin' on it, that's all."

Will studied the men closely and realized that they were telling the truth. They had the look of cowboys, in their faces and in their eyes. Also, their hands were callused from hard work. These weren't outlaws.

"Are there rooms back there?" Will asked, pointing toward the rear of the building.

"Yeah," Slim answered, laughing. "You wantin' to go back there?"

"If you do, ask ole' Scrub here which one of these girls is best. He knows 'em all," Dirk teased, and the others laughed at Scrub's expense.

"Anyone back there now?" Will asked. "Americans, I mean?"

"Ain't no other Americans here a'tall, 'cept just

what's sittin' around this table," Slim said.

"Why do you ask?" Dirk inquired.

"No reason in particular," Will answered. "I stopped down at the church to fill my canteen and the padre said five American men and one girl rode in today. I was just curious about them."

"Yeah, well, a group of them rode in today, but they didn't stay."

"No, they come in and bought a bottle then went right on. Weren't very friendly."

"Anyhow, they wasn't all Americans," Slim said.

"What?"

"They wasn't all Americans," Slim insisted. "Four of them was, and I think the girl was, but she stayed outside on her horse and didn't come in so I never got a good look at her."

"What color dress was she wearing?"

"It was red," Dirk said. "You fellas remember that 'cause Scrub said they weren't nofhin' no prettier than a woman in a red dress."

"I thought you didn't get a good look at her," Will said.

Slim laughed. "Scrub don't have to get a good look. To him all women is pretty, whether they be wearin' a red dress or not."

"The other man was Mex," Scrub said. "And he didn't ride out with the others, neither. Leastwise, I don't remember seein' him leave."

Will had no idea what made him look around at that precise moment. Maybe it was the fact that he had just learned that one of the men he was looking for was Mexican and he decided to look again at those in the bar. Or maybe he heard something. Or, maybe it was true, what they sometimes said of gunfighters, that they had a sixth sense about danger. For whatever reason, Will looked around, just as the Mexican against the wall was dumping the bargirl from his lap. She screamed in surprise and fright as the Mexican came up with a pistol in his hand.

"What the hell?" Slim asked. "You fellas look out!" He and the other cowboys dived for the floor, just as the Mexican fired.

Will brought his own gun up, even as the Mexican's gun burst the firing cap. The Mexican's bullet hit the deck of cards the cowboys had been playing with, sending them scattering.

The cowboys weren't the only ones on the floor. By now everyone else in the place had also dived for cover, leaving only Will and the Mexican standing. But the Mexican didn't stand for long because Will fired before the Mexican could pull the trigger a second time.

The heavy slug from Will's gun sent the Mexican crashing through a nearby table. Glasses and bottles tumbled and tequila spilled to merge with the blood which was already beginning to pool on the floor. The gun smoke drifted slowly up to the ceiling, then spread out in a wide, nostril-burning cloud. Will looked around the room quickly to see if anyone else might represent danger, but all he saw were the faces of the customers and they showed only fear, awe, and surprise.

"Damn!" Scrub said into the silence that followed the two gunshots.

"Was he the one with the Americans?" Will asked.

Dirk repeated the question in Spanish, and half a dozen of the Mexican customers nodded in the affirmative.

"Yeah, he was," Dirk said.

"Is he dead?"

Again the question was repeated in Spanish, and one of those who had hurried over to look at him, now nodded yes. "Si, Senor. He is dead."

"Damn. I didn't want to kill him," Will said. "I needed some information from him."

"You didn't want to kill him, huh?" Slim asked. He chuckled. "Well, you shot pretty straight for someone who didn't want him dead."

It was very late in the afternoon when Gid saw some horse droppings that told him they were gaining on Doran and the others.

Thirty minutes later, they came across a pass in the

rocks that was so narrow they could only ride in single file. As Gid was tracking, he went through the draw first. Just as he emerged on the other side, he was shot from ambush. He had not heard nor suspected anything until the moment the bullet hit him, a sudden, numbing, sledge-hammer blow to his arm that knocked him from his horse. Immediately after that, a man jumped out from behind a rock and charged after him, firing his pistol as he ran. The bullets hit the ground around him, ricocheted off the rocks, then sailed off, filling the canyon with their angry whine.

Gid had been hit in his left arm and that caused him to fall on his right side. He was lying on his right side and thus unable to get to his gun. Incredibly, that opportunity was all the assailant saw, and he closed to within three feet of Gid, so intent on finishing him off that he didn't even notice Will, who was just coming out of the draw.

"I've got you, Crockett! I've got you!" Bean yelled excitedly, pointing his pistol at Gid's head.

Will didn't have time to shout a warning. All he had time for was to pull the trigger. His bullet tore into the attacker's throat. Bean gagged, dropped his gun, and put both hands to his neck. Will shot again and this time his bullet hit him right in the middle of the face, tearing away his nose.

"Will!" Gid shouted. By now Gid had his own gun

out and he fired, even as he shouted. His bullet found its mark, and a second ambusher fell, his gun clattering down across the rocks before him.

As the man slid down, head first, Will looked around for more. He heard a horse riding away and he climbed, quickly, up onto the same rock from which the last man had been killed, to see if he could get a shot at the one who was running. It was too late. Whoever it was got away.

Will came back down from the rock, as Gid was looking at the two dead men.

"This is our old friend, Russ Bean," Gid said, pointing to the man with his nose shot away.

"He looks bad," Will said.

"Yeah," Gid agreed. "But, you have to admit, he never was all that good looking when he was alive." Gid took the bandanna from around his neck and began trying to tie it around his wound.

"Here, let me do that," Will said, finishing the task. He tightened the bandanna.

"Damn, don't be so rough. You're squeezing my arm in two," Gid complained.

"Have to," Will replied. "Otherwise you could bleed to death."

"That might be preferable to letting you doctor me," Gid teased.

Chapter Nineteen

Dottie and her captors had reached an old, deserted line cabin earlier that afternoon. Now Dottie lay on a filthy cot, her hands tied to what was left of the headboard and her feet tied to the broken footrail.

During the long afternoon, she had watched the dust mote-laden sunbeams as they crisscrossed throughout the darkened interior of the cabin, forming little spears of light to stab through the cracks in the walls and gaps and holes in the shake-shingled roof. Now the bright spears of light were gone, replaced by the dim glow of early evening.

When the outlaws came to the ranch, they had caught them totally by surprise, killing her mother and father, shooting down Leigh, even as he was shooting two of them. When they left the ranch, Dottie was their prisoner. There had been eight then, but three of the men broke away not too long after they left. Then another one of them, a Mexican, stayed back in the little Mexican town they had come through. After leaving the town, they rode hard, not even stopping to eat, until they reached this shack, which Doran had evidently known about. Now Doran was somewhat agitated that none of the men who had ridden off had returned.

"Maybe the Crocketts got 'em," one of the remaining men suggested.

"They couldn't have killed all four of 'em," Doran replied. "Hell, they didn't even know about the Mex. You want to know what I think? I think the bastards ran out on us."

"They wouldn't run out on us, Doran. Hell, I know Gray wouldn't," Armstrong said. "I'm tellin' you, some-thin' must've happened. Why don't you let me and Smitty and Bean go back and wait on 'em? We'll pick us out some place and kill the sons of bitches from ambush."

"All right, Armstrong you go on back," Doran agreed. "I'll wait for you here. But as soon as the bastards are dead you come back here and tell me, you hear? You come back here and tell me."

"We'll come back," Armstrong promised.

That had been over two hours ago and the men weren't back yet. As a result, Doran was pacing back and forth in the little cabin, going over to the window every couple of minutes to look outside.

"They aren't coming back," Dottie said.

"You," Doran said, turning away from the window and pointing at her, "just keep your mouth shut."

"I was just telling you what you already know," she said.

"I mean it," Doran said again. "Just keep your mouth shut or I'll gag you."

Dottie shut up, but she continued to watch Doran's every move, riveting him with her eyes. He broke out in a heavy sweat and kept wiping his face and the top of his head.

"Quiet!" he said a moment later, though she hadn't made a sound. "I hear someone." He drew his pistol and stood at the window, staring through it. Suddenly he turned around with a big grin on his face. "It's Armstrong," he said. "He's back. I guess you know what that means. The Crocketts are dead." He walked over and looked down at the cot. "Not much point in keepin' you around any longer now, is there?" he asked.

Dottie heard the horse stop out front, then the door opened and Armstrong came bounding in.

"They killed Bean and Smitty," he said.

"What? I thought you were going to shoot them from ambush."

"Hell, we did," Armstrong said. "Or at least, we tried

to. I hit the big one, I knocked him down off his horse. Then Bean, I don't know, he just went sort of crazy. Maybe it was because he thought I was goin' to get the credit or somethin'. Anyway, he just run out toward the big one, shooting wild, without even stopping to think that there was two of 'em. The other one come out of a draw then and shot Bean dead. Then that damn fool Smitty raised up and got himself shot dead too."

"But you said you got the big one, right? You said you knocked him off his horse."

"Yeah. I did."

"Well?"

"Well, what?"

"Did you kill him, man? Did you kill him?"

"No, I don't think so. I think I just winged him or somethin'."

"You don't think so," Doran said with a scornful snort.

"I know so. I didn't kill him," Armstrong said.

"All right. All right, then we'll just wait here for both of them."

"To hell with that. You wait for them," Armstrong said. "I ain't stayin' aroun' here. I've had enough. There ain't no way I'm goin' to go up against them Crocketts again."

"You ain't runnin' out on me!" Doran said.

"You think not? You watch me. And if you got any sense, you'll run too. Come on, leave the girl an' let's go."

"We're staying," Doran insisted.

"I'm not staying," Armstrong said. "I wouldn't even come back here 'ceptin' to warn you." Armstrong started for the door but before he reached it, there was a gunshot, then a billow of smoke filled the cabin. Armstrong spun around with a surprised look on his face. He saw Doran standing there, holding the smoking gun in his hand. Armstrong put his hand around to his back, trying to find the bullet hole, but he couldn't reach it. "You son of a bitch, you shot me!" he said.

Armstrong pitched forward onto his face. He tried to get back up, raised up to his hands and knees, then went down again. This time he lay still and after a couple of gasping breaths, he was dead.

"I told you," Doran said under his breath. "You wasn't leavin'."

The night air felt refreshingly cool after the long, hot day. Will dismounted and stared at the cabin, some one hundred yards away.

"You think that's them?" Will asked.

"This is where the trail leads," Gid replied.

"I'm going to go up and take a look. You hang on to the horses."

"Why don't we hobble the horses and I'll go with you?" Gid suggested.

"No, you stay here," Will insisted. "No offense, Little Brother, but you aren't all that good at sneaking around."

"All right," Gid agreed. "But if you need me, I'll be here."

Will nodded at his brother, then slipped through the shadows until he was on the outside of the cabin. He edged along the wall until he could look through a gap between the boards. Incredibly, there was a candle burning inside, thus allowing him to see what was going on.

Will saw Dottie staked out on the bunk, and two men in the front of the cabin, looking out through the two front windows. Doran was very animated, moving back and forth nervously, while the other man was absolutely still. There was something strange about the second person, but Will didn't know what it was.

The problem, as Will saw it, was that there was only one way into the cabin, and that was through the front door. And Doran had the front door so well covered that there was no way he could get in without affording the outlaw a clear line of fire.

The cabin was old and had probably been abandoned for a long time. That explained all the gaps in the wall, the collapsed porch, and the caved-in roof.

There were no windows at the back of the cabin, so Will went around behind, found the exposed beam of a rafter and used it to pull himself up onto the roof. Lying on his stomach he moved across the top of the cabin, slowly, quietly, testing the shingles until he could find several that were loose and rotten. He pulled one aside, then looked through. Doran was still pacing around nervously, but the other man had not moved since the first time Will saw him.

"Where is he?" Will heard Doran ask. "Why don't he come?"

"He's waiting for you to make a mistake," Dottie said.

"Shut up!" Doran replied, whirling around toward her. He pointed his gun at her. "The only thing keepin' you alive now is I might need you. But if you don't keep that mouth of yours shut, I'll shoot you whether I need you or not."

Will realized that Doran was getting very nervous, and the more nervous he got, the more dangerous it would be for Dottie. He had to do something and he had to do it soon.

Will studied the roof for a moment, then saw that there was one area which was covered by four or five rotten shingles. He could break them off easily, but if he did, Doran would surely hear him the moment he started.

Then he got an idea. He wouldn't break them off one at a time, he would break them off all at once. But the only way he could do that would be to jump right through them. And that meant a drop of eight to ten feet to the floor below.

Will stood up quietly, took a deep breath, then leaped right into the middle of the rotten shingles, and crashed through.

Dottie was as shocked as Doran when she saw Will suddenly burst through the roof and fall to the floor. She let out a little scream of surprise.

"What the hell!" Doran shouted, swinging around from the window to blaze away at the intruder. A long finger of flame spit from the end of his gun and the heavy slug tore into the floor where Will landed. It would have hit Will, had Will not rolled to his left the moment he fell. Will fired as he rolled, and Doran went down, clawing at a hole next to his heart. Will rolled again and turned his gun toward the second man, who still hadn't turned around.

"He's dead!" Dottie shouted.

Will, seeing that the second man was, indeed, dead, lowered his gun.

"Doran shot him when he thought he was going to run away," Dottie went on. "He stuck him up in the window to fool you into thinking there were two of them in here."

Will chuckled. "It worked," he said. "I was fooled." He put his gun away then, and went over to the cot to untie the ropes that held Dottie bound. "Are you all right?"

"Yes," Dottie said. As soon as she was untied, she

ringed Will's neck with her arms and hugged him hard. "Thank you," she said. "I knew you would come."

"It's all over now," Will said, gently. "Gid's outside. We'll take you back home."

"Home?" Dottie said. Tears came to her eyes. "What's there to go home to? Ma and Pa are both dead. So's Leigh. And the ranch is burned."

"The buildings are burned," Will said. "But the land is still there. So are the cattle." He smiled. "And so is Leigh."

"What?" Dottie gasped. "But I saw him ..."

"You saw Leigh shot," Will interrupted. "But he didn't die and he's not going to."

"Thank God," Dottie said, crying with relief.

"Have you had anything to eat?"

"No, not since I was captured."

"Why don't I get Gid in here to fix us something to eat? Then we'll rest here tonight and leave at first light."

Chapter Twenty

When Wilson Hays came across Bean and Smitty's bodies, he chuckled.

"Oh, you Crockett boys are good all right," he said to himself. "You're damn good. Maybe even the best around... next to me." He stood up and walked over to his horse and patted the polished stock of the Whitworth. "By this time tomorrow, I'll have both of you belly-down across your horses."

Hays had already heard the story, how Doran had burned out the Chamberlain Ranch, killed the girl's parents, and stolen the girl. Will and Gid Crockett had gone after her.

There were some back in San Pedro who figured the Crocketts had bitten off more than they could chew. Doran had at least half a dozen outlaws he could call upon. There were only two of the Crocketts.

Hays hadn't believed for one moment that the Crocketts were in over their heads. Then, as he began following the bloody trail they were leaving behind, he knew the Crocketts would find the girl. And once they found her, they would have to bring her back to San Pedro. All Hays would have to do is wait for them.

Some might wonder why Hays was so doggedly determined to bring the Crocketts in. After all, even after he killed them, he would have to get an affidavit signed by an officer of the court, verifying that they were dead, then he would have to present that affidavit to a court official in the state of Kansas.

Kansas might be the only place where a reward was still in effect, but the state of Kansas wasn't the only one who wanted them dead. The thing that had brought Hays here in the first place was a letter of employment. The terms of employment were very simple. All he had to do was kill Will and Gid Crockett.

Hays pulled out a piece of jerky and began chewing. He washed it down with a swallow of water, then hobbled his horse and threw out his blankets. May as well get some sleep, he thought. The Crocketts wouldn't be through there before tomorrow.

A hot dry wind moved through the canyon, pushing before it a billowing puff of red dust. The cloud of dust lifted high and spread out wide and made it look as if there were blood on the sun.

Four horses came into the canyon. Will, Gid, and Dottie were the three riders. Doran's cold, lifeless body was belly-down on the fourth horse.

It was mid-morning and they had been riding since first light. Now, with Doran and most of his henchmen dead, there didn't seem much need to keep on the razor's edge of alertness. That was good, because Gid was running a little fever from his arm wound and Will kept looking around at him every so often.

Gid chuckled. "You think I can't stay in the saddle, Big Brother?"

"I don't know," Will answered. "I'm thinking about tying you on your horse."

"Long as it's not belly-down like ole' Doran here," Gid replied.

Will wondered how his brother could keep going. He wasn't wounded, but even he could feel the weariness creeping in, and as he sat in the saddle and let the sun warm his back, his eyelids began to grow heavy and he let his guard down.

The heavy slug whizzed by him, less than an inch in front of his nose. It hit a rock then let out a banshee whine as it flew away. Will's hair stood on end and his stomach rose to his throat as he was instantly awake. The deep boom of a distant rifle shot reached his ears.

"It's Hays!" Will shouted.

"What?"

"Come on!" Will called, slapping his legs against the side of his horse and urging him off the trail. He jerked the reins on Doran's horse so that it, Gid and Dottie followed him.

There was a second shot and this time the bullet hit one of the spans of a pear cactus. The cactus exploded into little pieces.

"Get under there!" Will shouted, pointing to a rock overhang. They rode behind the cover just as a third shot was fired. Will swung down from his horse, reached up and literally pulled Dottie down. He shoved her head down behind a rock and he and Gid got down with her. They were safe there. Hays would have to come up on them to get a shot, and that would bring him into Will's range.

"Who'd you say that was?" Gid asked.

"Wilson Hays. You know ... the bounty hunter who killed Campbell? I think he's also the one who killed my horse."

"If he's a bounty hunter, why the hell is he after us? We aren't wanted in any state except Kansas."

"May not be a state," Will explained.

"What do you mean?"

"I have a feeling some individual has put a reward on us."

"Damn!" Hays said as he reloaded his rifle. He'd seen where the Crocketts and the girl ran and he knew he couldn't get a shot at them from there.

Hays stood up and stretched, took a few steps back from where he had been sitting, and dipped his hand down into the stream, then raised it to his mouth to take a drink. He laughed.

"How much water you folks got in your canteen?" he asked under his breath. "How long can you wait?"

Hays walked back over to his perch on the high rock and waited. The Crocketts and the girl would have to come out some time.

It was late in the afternoon when Hays saw them. At first he wasn't sure it was them, there was only a slight movement way down below. Then, as he looked closely, he saw what was going on.

Two riders were leaning low over the neck of their horses, moving slowly though a twisting ravine, behind an outcropping of rocks and a screen of mesquite. Hays hadn't noticed that possible escape route when he set up his ambush. They almost made it through, would have, perhaps, had it not been that Hays caught a flash of red, the girl's dress, out of the corner of his eye.

"Well now," Hays said. "Aren't you the clever ones? You've found a little ravine that leads out of there, haven't you?"

Hays looked around quickly, then saw another rock, perhaps a hundred yards away and fifty feet higher. It would make the shot more difficult, but he was sure that from that vantage point, he would be able to see them when they emerged at the far end of the ravine. And if he could see them, he could kill them.

Hays hurried to the new position. He had time, not only because the ravine twisted and turned for quite a ways until it ran out, but also because the two riders were moving very slowly so as not to attract his attention. As a result, he was in position, lying on his stomach, with the scope to his eye, when the two horses emerged.

"How come there is only one of you and the girl?" he asked. "Where's the other one?"

He looked around, very carefully, to make certain that the second brother wasn't sneaking up on him. When he was sure that he wasn't, he got back in position and waited for the riders to appear. He may have hit the other brother. At any rate, he would take care of him later. A bird in hand was better than two birds in the bush.

The moment the two riders came out of the ravine, the horses broke into a gallop.

"Ha!" Hays said. "Do you think you are clear?"

Hays aimed at the target, held it in his scope for a moment, then squeezed the trigger slowly. Even as he was rocked back by the recoil of the exploding cartridge he could see a puff of dust fly away from the back of Crockett's shirt. Crockett fell from his horse.

The girl's horse continued on for a few feet, then stopped and came back. Hays opened the breech and slipped in another shell. He thought about killing the girl too, then decided against it. He wasn't getting paid to kill her. He laughed, then hurried back to his horse, slipped the Whitworth back into the saddle sheath, and started the long ride down to claim his prize.

Money in the bank as soon as he delivered the body to San Pedro, then another $ 1,500 as soon as he managed to get verification of the killing to the proper authorities in Kansas.

But it wasn't just the money. No, sir. It was the satisfaction.

He recalled that time during the war, when one of the Crocketts was giving aid and comfort to the enemy. Considering that treasonous, he'd tried to stop him, but the other one had come up behind him and hit him on the head.

Yes, sir, he had waited a long, long time for this.

As Hays drew closer, he saw that the red dress was kneeling beside the body. What was the girl doing there? Why hadn't she ridden on while she had the chance? Maybe he should go ahead and kill her. He knew that the man who was paying him for Will Crockett also wanted the girl dead. He was the one who set up the raid on the girl's ranch in the first place. Maybe there would be a bonus for him if he brought in not only Crockett's body, but the girl's as well. He had never killed a woman before, but when he stopped to think about it, he didn't suppose it mattered all that much. Killing was killing.

Hays pulled his shotgun from the other saddle sheath, opened it to check the load, then snapped it shut. As he drew closer still, he urged the horse into a trot and raised the gun.

Suddenly the figure in red stood up and turned around to face Hays.

"What?" Hays gasped.

It wasn't the girl! It was Will Crockett, wearing the girl's dress! Almost as soon as he realized that, he saw, also, that Crockett had a gun in his hand.

Will fired and saw a puff of dust leap from Hays's shirt. Hays pitched back out of the saddle as the shotgun flew out of his hand. Will hurried over to look down at him. When he got there he saw that Hays was still alive, though only barely.

"You look awful funny in that dress," Hays said. His voice was strained.

"Yeah," Will said. "I wouldn't want to ride into town

like this."

"Pretty smart," Hays admitted. "Who ... who the hell did I kill?"

"Nobody," Will said. "He was already dead. That was Doran, wearing my clothes and my hat."

"I'll be a son of a bitch."

"Who you working for, Hays? Surely you didn't come this far on a Kansas warrant?'"

"Ain't you figured that out yet, Crockett? We been feedin' at the same trough." Hays began to laugh. "The same trough," he said. "That's good. That's real good." He laughed again, but the laughing changed to a spasmodic coughing, then he gasped once, and the breathing ended with one final death rattle.

"Is he dead?"

When Will looked up, he saw Gid and Dottie. Dottie was wearing only a petticoat and chemise, and she kept her arms across her breast, preserving some modesty, if not her dignity.

"Yeah," Will said. "He's dead. Now, what do you say we get back into our right clothes?"

"Oh, I don't know, Will ... I think you look just real nice," Gid teased.

As they were changing clothes, Will thought about what Hays said about them feeding at the same trough. Then he thought of something else that had been bothering him, though it had been at the very back of his mind until now.

"Dottie. On the morning Doran raided your ranch, why was your father home?"

"What do you mean, why was he home?"

"I thought he had to run over to Pantano that day."

"No."

"Are you sure?"

"Yes, of course I'm sure," Dottie said. "We were all waiting on the other ranchers to come over and help us put on a new roof that day." She laughed. "Anyway, Pa hated Pantano. He claimed the feed store over there cheated him. He'd go out of his way to avoid the place."

When the little party rode into San Pedro the next day, they attracted quite a bit of attention. A young boy saw them first and he went running back into town to shout the news. Others came out then and the crowd of citizens formed a parade as they ran along the street alongside the four horses.

"They brought the girl back safe," someone said.

"Who's that belly-down on the horse?" another asked.

"Why, that there's Doran."

"They done it! By gum, they cleaned 'em all out!"

Leigh met them about halfway through town, and though one arm was in a sling and he was getting along on crutches, he hobbled out into the middle of the street to greet Dottie. She slid down from her horse and ran to him.

"Will, Gid, thanks," Leigh said.

Will smiled at the young cowboy, then he saw his brother weaving back and forth in his saddle.

"Leigh, Dottie, do me a favor, will you? Get Gid to the doctor."

"No, I'm all right," Gid said. "A couple nights rest and I'll be fine."

"Couple nights more without getting that tended to, and you might be dead," one of the townspeople said, and he and another helped Gid down from his horse.

"Where you goin', Will?"

"I've got some business to tend to," Will answered.

Will continued on through town until he reached the Cattlemen's Association Building. From the horses and buggies gathered out front, he saw that a meeting was in session. That was good, that was just what he wanted.

Will pulled Doran's body off the pack horse, threw it across his shoulder, then packed it into the building.

"Crockett! You're back!" Stiles said. He had been sitting at the head of the table and he stood up as Will entered the room.

"I've got a package for you," Will said, dumping Doran's body onto the table. Several of the ranchers recoiled in horror.

"That's a rather gruesome package to deliver in here, isn't it?" Stiles scolded. "Couldn't you have just left him on the street?"

"I suppose I could have," Will said. "But I thought you might want to see him. You know, this means you'll have to get someone else now."

"Yes, I know, your work is all done," Stiles said. "But we won't need anyone else now."

"That's not what I'm talking about. I mean you, Doc Stiles, are going to have to get someone else to do your dirty work, now that your man, Doran, is dead."

"My man?"

"Look here, Crockett, what the Sam Hill are you talking about?" Woods asked.

"Yeah, that's what I'd like to know," demanded Stiles.

"What I'm talking about is the fact that Doran worked for Doc Stiles," Will said.

"What?" the others asked.

"How dare you say such a thing?" Stiles blustered. "Why, this is preposterous."

"Is it? Why did you hire Hays to kill my brother and me?"

"What makes you think I did?"

Will tossed a letter onto the table. "I took this off his body," Will said. "After he tried to kill me."

"What is that?" Holeman asked, as Woods picked it up.

Woods read the letter, then looked over at Stiles. "It's a letter," he said, "offering $2,500 to Hays for each of the Crocketts."

"Is that true, Doc?" Ashby asked.

"Well, what if it is? The Crocketts are wanted men. They rode with Quantrill. Kansas still has a reward out for them. I was just supplementing the reward, that's all. There's nothing illegal about that."

"But why would you want to do that? Crockett was cleaning out the rustlers for us."

"I haven't made any secret of the fact that I've been against all the killing," Stiles said. "I was just trying to stop it the only way I knew how, that's all." He looked at Will. "Now, if you think you can reason from that, that I was the head of this rustling operation, then I'd like to know how."

"Yeah, Crockett, that's a pretty far reach," Woods said. "How do you come up with such a conclusion?"

"I'll leave it up to you to figure out who has gained every time one of the other ranchers is forced out," Will said. "And I'll leave it up to you to find the missing cows somewhere on Stiles's land. But I do have one question for Stiles. Do you remember the meeting the other morning? The day Chamberlain's ranch was burned out? Who called the meeting?"

"Doc Stiles," Holeman said.

"I'm the President. It's my right to call the meetings," Stiles said.

"Yes, and you told the others that Chamberlain wouldn't be coming to the meeting because he was going to Pantano."

"That's what he told me."

"You're lying. You never told him about the meeting. And the only reason you called one was to make sure none of these men were out at Chamberlain's ranch when Doran and his bunch made their raid."

"You're crazy."

Will looked over at Woods and Holeman. "Think about it, men. Do you remember what you were supposed to do that morning?"

"The roof!" Holeman said. "We were going to help Chamberlain put on a new roof."

"Yeah," Woods said. "Why would he go to Pantano if..."

"Look out! Stiles has pulled a gun!" one of the men shouted.

Will spun around toward Stiles. He had been expecting this, had hoped for it in fact, and when he saw the gun in Stiles's hand he pulled his own, drawing and firing in the same, fluid, motion, doing it so quickly that the noise of his shot covered Stiles's so that they sounded as one, even though Stiles had fired a split second sooner.

Stiles's bullet whizzed by harmlessly, burying itself in the wall behind Will. Will's bullet caught Stiles right between the eyes. The president of the San Pedro Cattlemen's Association fell back with his arms flopping down to either side, and his head lolled back against the back of the chair. Both eyes were open but there was a third opening, a small, black hole, right at the bridge of his nose. Actually, only a small amount of blood trickled from the hole, though the chair-back cushion was already stained red with the blood that had gushed out from the exit wound.

The ranchers looked at Stiles's body in shock. It had all happened so fast that, for a moment, they could almost believe that it hadn't happened at all, that Stiles had merely sat back down in his seat. But the drifting cloud of acrid smoke said otherwise.

"Is he dead?'" Woods asked.

"As a doornail," someone answered.

Woods looked back toward Will, who had now put his gun away and was looking at Stiles with eyes that were totally devoid of expression.

"Mr. Crockett, I reckon we owe you some apologies," Woods said.

"No, Woods," Will said. "What you owe me is some money."

A Look At: Escape From The Devil
(The Crocketts Book 9)

WITH THE CROCKETTS' IN TOWN, EVERY TWO-BIT GUNSLINGER'S CHANCES OF SURVIVING ARE JUST ABOUT ZERO...

After brothers Will and Gid Crockett deliver several horses to Colonel John Abernathy – a man they knew during the civil war – he hires them to accompany his sixteen-year-old daughter, Julia, on a stagecoach trip for fear she may be kidnapped and held for ransom.

Julia is very highly sought after, and Silas King and his outlaw gang refuse to back down.

The Crockett brothers find themselves in the outlaw town of Jericho with nothing but a shootout standing in the way of justice.

"The Crockett brothers carry a mean punch and wild adventures."

AVAILABLE NOW

About the Author

Robert Vaughan sold his first book when he was 19. That was 57 years and nearly 500 books ago. He wrote the novelization for the mini-series Andersonville. Vaughan wrote, produced, and appeared in the History Channel documentary Vietnam Homecoming.

His books have hit the NYT bestseller list seven times. He has won the Spur Award, the PORGIE Award (Best Paperback Original), the Western Fictioneers Lifetime Achievement Award, received the Readwest President's Award for Excellence in Western Fiction, is a member of the American Writers Hall of Fame and is a Pulitzer Prize nominee.

Vaughan is also a retired army officer, helicopter pilot with three tours in Vietnam. And received the Distinguished Flying Cross, the Purple Heart, The Bronze Star with three oak leaf clusters, the Air Medal for valor with 35 oak leaf clusters, the Army Commendation Medal, the Meritorious Service Medal, and the Vietnamese Cross of Gallantry.

www.ingramcontent.com/pod-product-compliance
Lightning Source LLC
Chambersburg PA
CBHW011027260626
47153CB00020B/2973

* 9 7 8 1 6 4 7 3 4 7 7 4 1 *